"What can I tell you? Demons are wacky that way," Piper said. "They don't always play fair." She rattled her arms in their chains. Nothing doing. Firm as ever. "Your only hope is to let me out of here so my sisters and I can help you."

Caitlyn's expression was grim. "Even if I wanted to—which, for the record, I don't," she said emphatically, "I wouldn't be able to. Those chains are enchanted. I don't have the power to break them."

"Someone in your village must," Piper said, practically begging.

"But that's just it, Piper. We're nowhere near my village," Caitlyn said sweetly. "We're in Lexor's dungeon. He'll be here any minute. You're trapped in the Underworld, my dear."

CHANGELING PLACES

Charmed®

Published by Simon & Schuster

CHANGELING PLACES

An original novel by Micol Ostow

Based on the hit TV series created by

Constance M. Burge

SIMON SPOTLIGHT ENTERTAINMENT
New York   London   Toronto   Sydney

S|S|E

SIMON SPOTLIGHT ENTERTAINMENT
An imprint of Simon & Schuster Children's Publishing Division
1230 Avenue of the Americas, New York, New York 10020
® & © 2005 Spelling Television Inc. All Rights Reserved.
All rights reserved, including the right of reproduction in whole or in part in any form.
SIMON SPOTLIGHT ENTERTAINMENT and related logo are trademarks of Simon & Schuster, Inc.
Manufactured in the United States of America
First Edition 10 9 8 7 6 5 4 3 2 1
Library of Congress Control Number 2004108436
ISBN 0-689-87852-4

To Mom, Dad, and David—who put up with me
while I am under deadline.

Many thanks to Beth Bracken and everyone at
Simon Spotlight Entertainment for the
opportunity, and of course to Phyllis
Ungerleider for the green light.

Prologue

To the casual observer the deep cover of the woods was notable only for its thick, lush wildlife, the carpet of green, and the canopy of foliage draped gracefully across its topography. For the most part, the residents of the Pacific Northwest took for granted their access to the great outdoors, with its breathtaking views and health-imbuing fresh air. Fog and grayness were often met with the same indifference as the bright, brilliant sunlight.

They shouldn't have been. Fog and grayness were an invitation. An invitation, that is, for the various creatures of the woodland to emerge and wreak the havoc that they were so capable of and so well known for.

The elves were aware of this. Elves knew what lay in store deep within the cover of the woods. For that reason, their home was beyond secluded. It was tucked into a tiny corner camouflaged by thickets of greenery, but also cloaked in mystical protection. The elves knew of the dangers of the woods, and they were careful to take measures to guard themselves.

On this afternoon life in the elf village proceeded as usual. Within a series of interconnected cottages, skilled workers hammered away, while others cooked, cleaned, and otherwise oversaw the day-to-day goings-on among the clan. At the nursery an elf nanny named Caitlyn was putting her last charge down for a nap. The elf babies slept soundly, in sync with the late-afternoon lull in elf energy. Life was peaceful.

But that wasn't to last.

A sudden flash of blinding white light and a cloud of smoke signaled the impending events. Suddenly a shape appeared in the nursery. She cut an imposing figure, wearing a catsuit of a deep gunmetal shade, and with long, silver-streaked, jet-black hair trailing down her back. The suit was so tight it looked painted on. Her fingernails were long and silver, and her cheekbones—sharp enough to cut glass—shimmered with a cold sheen.

As if on cue, the babies began to shriek and wail from their bassinets.

Caitlyn instinctively grabbed the baby with which she'd been fussing and stepped back. "How did you get here?" she asked incredulously.

The woman looked at her witheringly. "Please. Anyone with a scrying crystal and access to superficial magic could find this village. Note to elves: Upgrade your protection cloak." She managed to look both incredibly imposing and astoundingly bored all at the same time.

"What do you want?" Caitlyn demanded with as much authority as she could manage.

"Your babies," the woman said flatly. "I am Mya, bounty hunter to the dark forces. A major presence in the Underworld wants your off-spring." She swept her gaze across the nursery and wrinkled her nose disapprovingly. "Not sure why."

Caitlyn straightened herself up haughtily, wanting to defend the elf young, but then realized the meaning behind the woman's words. "Our children? Who?" she asked in a panicked voice.

"Does it matter?" Mya asked simply. "As long as I get paid, I don't get involved. But I don't get paid unless I bring back the goods." She reached a slender, pale arm to a baton that swung from the belt of her jumpsuit.

Whatever the baton did, Caitlyn was guessing it probably wasn't good. "Wait!" she shrieked. "Maybe we can work something out."

Mya shrugged. "I don't care how we do this, but it's going to get done."

Mind racing, Caitlyn grasped for straws. "If you don't care, then you won't mind if I try to find you another solution. Please," she begged, near tears, "I love these children. I couldn't let you take them from us."

Mya stood silently, watching Caitlyn. Fearing the woman's growing irritation and impatience, Caitlyn rushed on. "We're elves. You know what powers we possess, what we're capable of," she reminded Mya feverishly. "We can find you human babies by switching ours for theirs. No one will know the difference. We will get you babies. Just not ours."

Mya nodded slowly, appearing to contemplate the offer. "Changelings," she mused aloud.

"Yes! Exactly!" Caitlyn agreed quickly. "Human babies."

"Human babies are of no use to my client," Mya said. "He is looking to raise an army. Humans are weak and mortal."

"Not if he empowers them mystically," Caitlyn argued. "Easily done. Humans with superpowers would be much more effective than elves—bigger, stronger, and more capable," she finished, swallowing back her guilt at speaking against her own. *Self-defense,* she reminded herself.

Mya tapped her silver fingertips against her belt in thought. "I don't normally stray from the parameters of my assignments," she commented.

It didn't sound quite like a no, so Caitlyn dared to hold her breath.

"But," she continued, "you make a good point. An army of humans . . . *magical* humans," she clarified, "would certainly be an asset to my client. He seems the type who might be into 'thinking outside the box.'" Her eyes lit up at the prospect of a higher bounty in exchange for the upgrade in personnel.

"So we have a deal?" Caitlyn asked eagerly, relieved. "You'll let me find you humans?"

"I'll let you try," Mya confirmed. "No promises. It depends on what you manage to bring back."

"Absolutely," Caitlyn said breathlessly. "I'll get you a nice sampling."

Mya leaned forward, peering skeptically at the elf nanny. "Why the willingness to go ahead with this plan? You'd be sacrificing human babies. I thought elves were creatures of good."

The nanny flushed. She'd had the same thought herself. She would have to run this plan by Rowan, the ruler of her clan, and his team of trusted advisors of course. But she was sure that they'd see things her way. *Desperate times, desperate measures . . .* , she repeated to herself.

She steadied her gaze, determined not to show her hesitance to the hard-edged bounty hunter. "You leave me no choice. I cannot let you take the young of my clan."

"Make no mistake—there are no guarantees," Mya insisted, "until I see the humans. I reserve the right to stick to my original plan if I so choose."

"Of course," Caitlyn said. "How would I stop you, after all?"

"Exactly," Mya said, sounding ominous. "You've got three days. I'll come back here to see what—or whom you've managed to come up with. And then, one way or the other, I will collect my targets, return to the Underworld, and, finally, collect my bounty."

"Three days will be fine," Caitlyn said. "No problem at all. I know exactly where to find babies."

Chapter One

"Have you had a muffin?" Piper Halliwell asked her sister Phoebe, sliding a basket of still-warm pastries onto the kitchen table just under Phoebe's nose.

"Huh? Um, no," Phoebe said, barely glancing up from her newspaper. She frowned. "You know I can't eat this early. I'm pretty much useless before my first cup of coffee." She pushed her reading glasses farther up her nose and flipped the front page of the arts section over.

Sunday mornings were generally low key in Halliwell Manor, but this was not the response that Piper had been hoping for. "Fine, but you're missing out. Freshly baked," she half sang, hoping to tempt Phoebe into reconsidering. Not happening. Her sister didn't even blink.

"Earth to Phoebe. What could possibly be so interesting in that newspaper that you are in no way able to even pretend you're listening to me?" Piper teased. "If you really can't eat my muffins, at least have some fresh-squeezed OJ. You know—breakfast, most important meal of the day, yadda yadda. . . ."

Sighing, Phoebe finally pushed the paper aside to look at her sister. "First of all, it's Sunday. So I'm not really needing a huge energy boost for all of the lying around—and possibly shopping—that I'm planning for my afternoon. And as for my interest in the paper, the *Chronicle* has a new advice columnist and I wanted to see what she's all about."

"Checking out the competition," Piper said, nodding. "Gotcha." Phoebe was a columnist for the San Francisco *Bay Mirror*—and a wildly popular one at that. Of course, her driven nature was probably at least part of the key to her success.

Phoebe grinned sheepishly. "Is it wrong that I'm feeling a little competitive?"

Piper couldn't resist a small chuckle. "A *little* competitive? Phoebes, if you weren't competitive, you wouldn't be the successful columnist that we know and love so well. No, it's not wrong. In fact, it's totally natural. And probably keeps you on top. But you know you have nothing to worry about, right? I think the only way you'd increase your fan base at this point would be by doing another photo spread," she joked, referring to an ill-advised moment when Phoebe had let her ambition get in the way of her . . . better judgment.

Phoebe laughed. She couldn't argue with Piper's logic. But that didn't change the fact that she had larger issues on her mind. She took a quick sip of coffee and said, "Trust me, being in the spotlight is amazing. I'm starting to really like it. But I'm definitely feeling the pressure of staying at the top of my game."

"I read your last column. Take it from me—you're at the top of your game, and you're not going anywhere," Piper assured her.

"Who's at the top of their game?" Paige Matthews asked, padding into the kitchen bleary eyed, still wearing a bright pink tank and some shorts that she had obviously slept in. Her hair was pulled into a messy ponytail. "Obviously not me, right at this moment. Caffeine, please," she said, rubbing her eyes and crossing to the coffeemaker before anyone else could offer to get it for her.

"Check this out," Piper said, eager for a new taste tester. "Fresh-squeezed orange juice and banana-nut muffins. Tell me you're hungry."

"Ugh," Paige groaned. "I made the bad mistake of eating a pint of ice cream before bed. My stomach is mad at me. I think just some toast for right now."

Piper made a face. "Fine, then. That's the last time I slave away in the hot kitchen for you two," she joked.

"Why the sudden burst of Martha Stewart?" Phoebe asked. Piper was a former chef, and as such, she was generally known for turning out culinary masterpieces on a whim, but the recent birth of her baby, Wyatt, had sapped most of her free time and definitely the bulk of her energy.

"Actually," Piper said, "I was inspired. Because all kidding aside, this just may very well be the last time I *can* slave away in a hot kitchen for you. I'm not sure how much time I'm going to have in the near future." Resigned to the idea that no one was going to be partaking of her baked goods, she plucked a muffin from the basket for herself and plopped down next to Phoebe at the table, biting in. "Mmmm, you're missing out," she commented as an afterthought.

"Very cryptic," Phoebe said. "Are you running away to join the circus? Because you know, it's harder to walk in those big clown shoes than you'd think."

"I don't even want to know how you know that," Paige said with a sideways glance at her big sister.

"Not to worry, I'm not breaking up the Power of Three," Piper answered. This was a veiled reference to Phoebe's recent decision not to follow her boss and long-distance boyfriend, Jason, to Hong Kong, in favor of sticking around the Manor and helping her two sisters kick demon butt. A decision, she had no doubt, was right. But that didn't make her miss Jason any less.

Piper continued. "No, the thing is," she said slowly, "now that Wyatt is getting a little older, I think . . . I think it's time for me to start thinking about going back to work. I mean, I think it's time for me to go back to work. Tomorrow," she clarified hastily. She flushed. She couldn't help it. She felt slightly guilty at the prospect of leaving Wyatt alone—more than slightly, truth be told—but she also needed to actively manage her club, P3. Piper was starting to feel a little bit not like herself. She needed to be Wyatt's mother, but she also needed to have her career back. *This is the twenty-first century*, she reminded herself for the millionth time. *Women can have families and careers at the same time. I can do this.* There was no reason that she shouldn't have it all.

But that didn't mean that she didn't feel bad about it.

Or worry about what her sisters would think. Their faces displayed no visible disapproval, though they both looked somewhat surprised. Piper couldn't decide whether that was a good thing or not. "Please say something, guys," she begged. "The fish eye is creeping me out."

"Piper, honey, that's great news," Phoebe said, giving her full attention to her sister at last. "It's just—well, I wasn't expecting it so soon, I guess. But if you're ready, that's all that matters." She paused. "*Are* you ready? Because it would be okay if you weren't. There aren't any hard-and-fast rules to the working-mother gig. You need to do what's best for you. And for Wyatt."

"You think it's too soon?" Piper asked, feeling nervous.

"It's a *little* soon," Paige admitted, stirring her spoon in her coffee mug. "But good soon. I mean, if you worked for some big corporation, your maternity leave would probably be over by now, right? The good news is that you're self-employed and you can jump back in whenever feels most comfortable for you."

Piper sighed. Her sisters seemed slightly worried, but she knew they had her best interests at heart. People kept telling her how hard it was to be a working mother. Was she biting off more than she was ready to chew?

"What sort of hours were you thinking?" Phoebe asked, frankly curious.

"I'm not sure," Piper said. "I figured I would go in for the afternoon tomorrow and see how it goes." She bit back the urge to tell them that she had actually been planning on going in every day that week. She had a feeling that would mark her as "overeager."

"Okay, I know that face," Phoebe noted, resting her chin in her hand and peering at her sister with scrutiny. "What are you not telling us?" She gasped and sat up straight. "You're going to go right back to full time, aren't you?" she asked. "Full steam ahead!"

Piper waved her hand dismissively. "How hard could it be?" she asked, ignoring her own nagging doubts. "Lots of women balance work and family. If they can do it, I can do it."

"If the letters I've been getting are any indication, Piper, honey—it's plenty hard," Phoebe insisted.

"Yeah, and those women aren't Charmed Ones," Paige pointed out. "You've got the whole protecting Innocents thing to worry about in addition to the basic pressures of a working mother."

"Well, look, I guess there's no guarantee that it will work out," Piper conceded, "or that it won't be harder than I'm making it out to be, but I have to try. I mean, like I said, lots of women do this, and they seem to do fine. And I think the only way to make it work is just to go for it. So that's what I'm going to do!"

"What does Leo think?" Phoebe asked.

"He worries, of course," Piper said. "But he thinks it's my decision and that I have to see what's going to work best for me. He's going to watch Wyatt for me while I'm out."

"Isn't he busy with a charge?" Paige pointed out.

Piper frowned. "Yes, but he's supposed to be back by tomorrow."

"But he might not be," Paige pressed.

Piper sighed. "This is true. These are the trials and tribulations of being an all-powerful witch married to a Whitelighter. What can I say?"

"Say, 'Paige, you're a lifesaver!'" Paige said, suddenly brimming with energy.

"Huh?" Piper asked, looking at her sister questioningly.

"Well, I know exactly who can watch Wyatt during the day tomorrow—me!" Paige said enthusiastically.

"Um, not that I don't appreciate the offer, but aren't you working tomorrow?" Piper asked.

Paige crossed her arms over her chest. "Yes. Doesn't *anyone* pay any attention to me around here?" she said, pretending to be frustrated. "I just started a new job last week. In a *day care center*," she added pointedly.

"Oh, yeah!" Phoebe nodded, smiling with recognition. "You told us that. And that kid kept picking his nose—"

"Not the point," Paige said, cutting her off.

"But I was listening," Phoebe said, self-righteous. "I do listen." She sipped at her coffee emphatically.

"Anyway, half the reason I even took the job was so that I could have some extra kiddie-care practice," Paige explained. "If you're going into the club during the day, and Leo is busy, it makes perfect sense."

Piper hesitated. Everything her sisters were saying was true, but something about the words "day care" gave her pause. It was just the last little added drop of guilt that she really could do without. She looked upward. "Leo!" she called, summoning her husband.

Momentarily the kitchen of the Manor was

bathed in a shimmer of lights, as Piper's husband, Leo Wyatt, orbed in. The lights dissipated and Leo smiled at his wife and sisters-in-law. "What's going on?" he asked.

"I was just telling Piper that I'd love to take Wyatt to the day care center with me tomorrow when I go in to work," Paige said, grinning.

"What day care center?" Leo asked, confused.

Paige glared at him. "The one I've been working at since last week, remember?"

"Of course," Leo said quickly. "Sorry, Paige. It's just that I've been really busy."

"And, I'll bet you could use an extra day or two with your latest charge," Phoebe chimed in, waving her hand at him enthusiastically. "All the more reason for Paige to take Wyatt to the day care center."

Leo glanced at Paige gratefully. "Would you?" he said. "I think it'll be good for him to play with other babies, and I'll feel more comfortable if Wyatt is with you. I'm sure he'd rather hang out with kids than be with us all the time. Toys, noise, *and* Auntie Paige? It's perfect. Don't you think it's perfect?" Leo said, turning to Piper eagerly.

Piper shrugged. "Day care. Isn't that just another way of saying, 'bad mother'?" she asked.

"No, I think it's synonymous with 'working mother,' which is what you're determined to be," Phoebe corrected, patting her sister's arm with affection. "Come on. Sooner or later, you'd have to give day care a try. At least this way it's with someone you trust."

"This way, it's with family," Paige insisted. "It's no different from me being *home* with Wyatt—in fact, it's even better, because this way Wyatt will be around other babies!"

"Even infants as young as he is?" Piper asked dubiously.

Paige nodded. "Yup. Totally. And there's an 'infant room' with a trained RN on staff and everything. Seriously, Piper—do you think I would take Wyatt somewhere that wasn't good for him?"

Piper glanced at her sister and saw the earnestness etched across her lovely features. Leo, too, was looking at Piper expectantly, and it was clear that Phoebe thought the idea was a good one. And why not, after all? She'd never think twice about leaving Wyatt home in the Manor with Paige. *And given all the demon activity that the Manor has seen*, Piper thought wryly, *he's gotta be safer in day care.*

"All right," she said, breathing heavily. "You win. Day care it is, starting tomorrow."

Day care, Phoebe thought to herself. *A viable option.*

After breakfast she had dragged her laptop off to her bedroom so that she could work in peace. She hadn't admitted as much to Piper, but she was more nervous than she would have liked about her column. Not that Phoebe doubted herself as a writer, but lately she'd been getting a rash of letters from a community she wasn't sure she was meant to serve: new mothers.

> *Dear Phoebe—*
> *My husband and I are involved in an ongoing headache, and I hope you can help! You see, our baby daughter was born two months ago, and my maternity leave is up very soon. I'd love to stay home and care for her, but unfortunately we need my salary to get by. I'm told that day care in San Francisco is reliable. Do you know if this is true? Or, perhaps you can tell us what to be on the lookout for when choosing a day care center? I wouldn't even know what questions to ask. And don't tell me to ask my friends, because none of them have babies yet!*
> *—Alone and Unsure*

Phoebe reread Alone's letter for the umpteenth time. Ironically, when Wyatt was born, Phoebe had gotten so into being Auntie that people at work had asked whether *she* was the baby's mother! But the truth was, while she was totally devoted to her adorable nephew, being his aunt was completely different from being his primary caregiver, and Phoebe found herself at a loss for how to help all of these mothers looking for guidance. Caring as she did for Wyatt, she was hypersensitive to the possibility of saying the wrong thing to her readers. What did she know about day care?

Well, I'll know something more by this time tomorrow, she told herself. *When Paige comes home from her day with Wyatt and gives me a rundown.*

She had to admit, she was slightly jealous. Piper was Wyatt's mother, and she and her baby had an unbreakable bond. And now Paige was going to be taking care of him all day long. Phoebe knew there was room enough for them all to love Wyatt, but she wished she had a specific, designated role too. *And not just "lady who observes him for her job," or "oddly overobsessed aunt,"* she thought.

Phoebe vowed to hit the bookstores on her lunch hour Monday. She needed some baby books, and fast.

She saved her notes on her computer and shut it down. She knew better than to try to force herself out of writer's block. The words would come when she was ready. In the meantime, well . . . she had other things on her mind. Like the slightly unsettled feeling in her stomach. When had she become so unqualified to give advice on babies? She had been by Piper's side all through her sister's pregnancy and was helping to raise the baby. She should have been a natural at this stuff. But there was something else bothering her. Something about the green eyed monster slithering its way up the insides of her belly. She knew feeling left out was silly. Immature, even. But that didn't make the feeling go away. Piper was Wyatt's mom. And now, Paige had a special role—even if it was temporary. Phoebe, however, was "only" Wyatt's aunt.

Since when was being Wyatt's aunt not special enough?

"Where do you want the champagne glasses?"

"Mmmm," Piper said, distractedly punching numbers into her calculator.

"Lady," a gruff voice said, "that's not an answer."

By way of emphasis, a large box of what Piper had to assume were champagne glasses were laid down at her feet with a dangerous-sounding *thunk*.

"Hey!" she protested, annoyed. "That's glass, you know."

"Yeah, and it's heavy," the delivery man said, sounding cranky.

"Let's just hope it's not broken," Piper snapped, grabbing at a letter opener from her office desk and lowering herself to the floor next to the box. She ripped into the cardboard and fished out a fluted glass, which was, thankfully, intact. "You're lucky," she said, waving the glass at the delivery guy. He didn't seem especially threatened by her tone.

"Yeah, and I'm also waiting for payment."

"What?" Piper asked, rising again and brushing a stray lock of chestnut hair out of her eyes. "Where's the rest of the shipment?"

The delivery man sighed and hitched his pants up at the waist. "In the front of the club. Like I said while you were in some kind of, like, trance."

"You try wading through months of backed-up paperwork," Piper said defensively. "You hire a temporary staff to cover your maternity leave—which, may I add, was abbreviated—but do they use your color-coded filing system? No, of course not . . ." Seeing the look the delivery guy was giving her, she trailed off. *Okay, that's it, I'm officially insane,* she decided. What was she doing explaining herself to him, anyway? "Never mind," she finished, feeling limp and washed out. "Give me your invoice. What's one more on the pile?"

The delivery guy grunted at her and fished the bill from his frayed pockets. He unfolded it and squinted at the smudged figures printed on the paper, smoothed the page out as best he could, and passed it to Piper. She took it from him, trying desperately not to shrink away from his grimy grip.

"Thanks," she said, glancing it over to be sure that the figures were correct. The numbers swam across the slip of paper. No doubt about it, she was shot from too many hours hunched over her calculator and her computer screen. "I'll be sure it's processed right away." She gestured to the mess of papers floating across her desk, the topmost of which were secured in place by a stapler that had seen better times.

The delivery guy shrugged. "Sure. Thirty days." He turned and left the office.

Piper didn't bother to follow him out. She sat back down in her chair, determined to process all of the last month's billing. Unfortunately, her calculator had other ideas. No matter how many numbers she punched, the club's income versus overhead could not be reconciled. *What am I missing?* she thought, not a little bit desperately. She'd been staring back and forth between her logs and her spreadsheets for several hours, and her brain had long since deteriorated to mush. She glanced at her watch: 5:00 PM. Wyatt's first day of day care was officially finished. *And I haven't been able to accomplish a single thing since I've been here*, she thought ruefully.

Sure, Piper had gone through the motions, but she'd been distracted and fuzzy. Granted, the billing was in lousy shape, but that didn't account for nearly a whole day lost. And she hadn't even glanced at the music lineup for the next month. She didn't want to think what sort of disasters lay in store for her on that count.

"Piper, we're here!" called a chipper voice from the front of the club. "And, ouch!" followed by the sound of glass shattering. "Oops."

Piper leaped up from her desk and ran to greet her sister and son. "Paige! How is Wyatt? And what did you break?" she asked, narrowing her eyes suspiciously. She scooped the boy from Paige's arms and covered his face with noisy kisses. "Did you miss Mommy today? Did you? Did you?" she cooed.

"Even if he could talk, Piper, he wouldn't have a chance to get a word in," Paige commented wryly. "And yes, I'm sure he missed you."

"Why? Did he cry all day?" Piper asked, looking up from Wyatt. "Did he cry some of the day? Did he cry at all—"

"*Relax.* No, not at all," Paige assured her. "He was great. Went right down for his naps, ate his lunch and all of his snacks, and even managed to avoid those toxic poops that he seems to think are so funny."

"So how did you know he missed me?" Piper asked, bouncing him on her hip. She had to admit to herself that he didn't look especially traumatized.

"Because the books assure me that he did," Paige said. "In a healthy way, of course. Why—are you disappointed that he did well today?"

"No!" Piper insisted. "Well . . . maybe," she offered after a moment. "I'm glad he behaved for you. I guess maybe I'm a little jealous. He probably did better than I did this afternoon." She gestured to the main room of P3 and its various areas of disarray. "I was a disaster.

Completely scatterbrained. I forgot all about a delivery of champagne glasses—"

"*Broken* champagne glasses," Paige corrected, tapping the box she had tripped on with her foot.

"Yes, thanks," Piper said sarcastically. She continued, "The billing is a mess, and I can't for the life of me figure out what the temp staff did to my filing system. Even if I was totally focused I would have had trouble."

"But I'm guessing you *weren't* 'totally focused'?" Paige hedged gently.

"Look at me," Piper said, gesturing with her free arm. "Sometime around three I took a bath in margarita mix."

"Ooooh," Paige murmured sympathetically, wrinkling her nose. She appraised the stains on Piper's jeans. "I bet those'll come right out."

"All I can say is, it better get easier," Piper said.

Wyatt yanked on a clump of her hair and laughed maniacally.

"Ow," Piper said wearily, as Paige leaned forward to remove his chubby fingers from her hair. "At least one of us had a good day."

Paige took another glance at the club. "Well, I'm sure you made a good start, in any case. Maybe you were taking on too much too soon?"

"Maybe," Piper admitted, though she hated to think that way. Since when had she ever been anything other than *uber*organized and totally on top of things? How was she going to adjust to being anything else?

"Grab your bag from the office and shut down your computer. Cut your losses. This will all be here tomorrow. We'll be bums tonight. I'll call for Thai and we'll binge on reality TV. We should just probably move this stuff"—she indicated the ten boxes of glasses stacked on the ground in front of her—"out of the doorway. Though I'm not sure how we're going to do it without giving ourselves hernias."

"What?" Piper shrieked in utter despair. "They were supposed to leave a dolly!"

"Where were you when they dropped the stuff off?" Paige asked.

"Uh, in the office, drowning in paperwork. How are we going to lift this stuff? If we're not careful, it's all going to break," she said.

"I wouldn't worry about that," Paige assured her. Seeing Piper's questioning glance, she prompted, "You know—since some of it already has?"

Piper shrugged and sighed heavily. Really, what else was there to do?

Chapter Two

"Okay, tell me the truth—isn't Wyatt just the cutest baby you've ever had in the center, like, *ever*, of all time?" Paige asked, her brown eyes widened in a picture of earnestness.

Dori, the head of the Bayside Child Care Center, gave her an are-you-kidding-me look. "Yes, Paige. The cutest. Ever. Of all time," she intoned robotically. Paige got the sense that it was a question Dori had fielded before.

"So, I guess I'm not the only proud auntie to grace the halls of the center, huh?" Paige questioned, smiling. "No big shock, really."

Dori bounced Wyatt on her hip, watching him shake a plastic rattle enthusiastically. "Well, he is a sweetie, I'll give you that," she conceded. "A lot more peaceful than a bunch of these newborns," she said, tilting her head discreetly in the direction of a particular bassinet toward the back of the room. "All babies are equally sweet and well behaved," she said in the same mechanical tone she had used before. She winked at Paige. "That's the party line here, anyway."

"Only if you've got the patience of a saint, which, I'm sorry to say, I don't think I do," Paige said, blowing a wisp of stray hair from her forehead and leaning heavily against the wall. She folded her arms across her chest. "Honestly, Dori, you've been here, what—ten years? I have to give you credit. I don't know how you do it. I get tired just watching these kids *nap.*"

It was true, Paige realized, even as the words came out of her mouth. She'd barely been on the job a week and she was already bone tired. Mentally and physically exhausted. Since she'd decided to go back to work she'd held down a string of varied temp jobs, some more demanding than others, but nothing compared to the rigors of spending an entire eight hours running after small children. And it didn't seem to matter how old they were either. The babies needed constant feeding, changing, and soothing when they cried. The toddlers needed minute-to-minute supervision, since they were prone to sticking their fingers anywhere, or shoving into their mouths whatever they happened to find on the ground. The older kids needed less supervision, to be sure, but they were amazingly high-maintenance nonetheless. Paige had never heard so much, "Paige, can you tie my . . ." or "Paige, can I have my . . ." or "Paige, so-and-so says . . ."

in her life. Until now, she hadn't realized just how complicated life could be for a four-year-old. She suddenly had a newfound appreciation for her parents for seeing her from infancy through to her days of teenage rebellion.

You're doing this for Wyatt, she reminded herself. Once she had fully assessed the demands of her job, she had adopted that phrase as her mantra. Paige's job would benefit herself, her sister, and her nephew. That made dealing with all of the dirty diapers, runny noses, and misplaced toys worthwhile.

Even if she was *dying* for a coffee break.

"Don't sell yourself short, Paige," Dori said reassuringly. "It takes a while to get the hang of watching after all of these kids. Honestly—after Paul threw up on you yesterday, I'm amazed you even wanted to come back!"

Paige shuddered at the memory. "Yeah, that was . . . fun," she said, thinking, *not so much.* Outside in the main play area, Paul was feverishly rolling across the floor in his go-chair, shrieking like the devil. Paige hoped against hope that he hadn't just eaten breakfast, or someone was in for a repeat performance of yesterday. *Just don't let it be me,* she begged the heavens silently.

"I'm going to see if I can get Wyatt down for a nap," Dori said, unwrapping his thick little fingers from her shoulders and placing him into the bassinet that had been designated his own.

"Why don't you go outside and see if Katie needs any help with the rest of them?"

"Sure," Paige said, peeling herself—somewhat reluctantly—from against the wall and heading out of the infant room and back into the main fray. She was sorry to leave. The babies were enjoying a rare moment of unified silence, and Paige mostly wanted to spend her time with her nephew. Paige took a deep breath and pushed the door open. The air was immediately filled with the sound of high-pitch giggles and singsong voices. And wailing. That was another sound. If Paige had thought that Wyatt had marathon lungs, she had been wholly unprepared for the cacophony of a host of overtired four-year-olds.

"Okay, folks, what's the problem?" Paige called out dutifully. She glanced over at Katie, the diminutive nurse with an amazingly large voice, who was hovering over a group of preschoolers engaged in a very involved game of house.

"CAN WE PLEASE JUST CALM DOWN?" Katie shouted. Paige could almost see the sound waves floating up in the air above her head.

Paige crossed over to what appeared to be the heart of the commotion, where one small boy, Jonathan, sat hunched on the carpet. His eyes were red, as if he had been crying. Paige kneeled down so that she and Jonathan were at eye level. "Hey, buddy, what's wrong?" she asked, smoothing his hair off his forehead. "I thought 'house' was supposed to be a pretty low-pressure game."

"I don't like the way *she* plays it," he said crossly, removing his thumb from his mouth to point an accusatory finger at the guilt-ridden face of a young girl with large, round brown eyes.

"Natalie, why don't you tell me how you play house," Paige suggested gently, "so that I can understand what's gotten Jonathan so upset."

Natalie nodded sadly, her brown braids bobbing up and down as her head moved. "I was going to be the mommy, and Devon was going to be the daddy. And then Jonathan was going to be the baby," she explained.

"And Jonathan didn't want to be the baby?" Paige guessed. She could remember hating to be the baby when she was younger. There was no prestige in being the baby, after all.

Jonathan shook his head in emphatic disagreement. "Nuh-uh. I don't mind. The baby doesn't have to do anything," he pointed out— rather astutely, Paige thought fleetingly. His eyes darkened. "But then she wanted us to have a fairy in the house. A pet fairy. Like *Tinkerbell*," he said, his voice thick with derision. "Everyone knows that fairies aren't real."

Uh, everyone except for witches, I guess, Paige thought. How to explain to Jonathan that in fact, magic was all around them, every day? *That's easy, Paige—you don't*, she reminded herself. As a

Charmed One, her job was to protect Innocents from evil, *not* to make them aware of the existence of magic in the first place. After all, most humans wouldn't accept the presence of the supernatural anyway. And those that were aware of it were usually given powers that enabled them to cope with their knowledge. Most ordinary humans were better off not knowing. Paige and her sisters knew this; in fact, each had learned it the hard way at one point or another.

"True, Jonathan, most people don't believe in fairies," Paige said carefully, doing her best to avoid outright lying to him while not actually admitting to any awareness of the existence of magic. "But sometimes it's fun to pretend," she said. "After all, playing house is a game of pretend anyway, right? So why not imagine that there's a fairy living in the house? It could be fun—like having a pet dragon or something!" she offered brightly. Boys liked dragons, didn't they?

Jonathan looked at her as if she was insane. "We could have a *dog*," he said. "Fairies are for *girls.*" With that proclamation, he scooped an action figure off the ground and stomped away to where a group of children were happily scribbling on construction paper, all thoughts of house, magical or otherwise, entirely forgotten.

Once Jonathan was gone, the rest of the group dispersed. Paige was able to determine that, in fact, most of the kids were upset at being forced to entertain the notion of fairies and any other nonconventional entities in their "house." *Pretty closeminded bunch*, she thought ruefully. Then she remembered back to how unreceptive she'd been when her half sisters first approached her and informed her of her powers. *Unreceptive? Try total denial!* she chided herself. But then again, kids were different . . . weren't they? Kids were all about creativity and imagination.

Paige turned to Natalie, who looked devastated at the outcome of her game. "Don't worry about it," Paige said, wrapping an arm around the girl's tiny waist. "Sometimes boys are weird," she went on. "I don't think there's anything wrong with pretending there's a fairy in your house."

Natalie shrugged. "I shouldn't have tried to make him," she said, more to herself than to Paige. "I shouldn't have talked about fairies."

"Hey, there's nothing wrong with using your imagination," Paige insisted. "Honestly."

Natalie shook her head. "My parents say I have too much imagination."

"What?" Paige asked in disbelief. "I mean, your parents, sure—they love you and I'm sure they know what's best—but Natalie, sweetie, it's a *good* thing to use your imagination! Seriously!"

Natalie shrugged. "But when I tell my parents about the things I see, they tell me I'm silly." Suddenly she looked nervous. "Don't tell them about how Jonathan cried about the fairy. They'll be mad."

Paige didn't want to deceive anyone, and giving daily feedback to the parents was part of her job. But she didn't see the harm in sweeping this incident under the rug. Especially since the whole thing seemed totally innocent. Paige had no idea why Natalie's parents would be so opposed to her using her imagination, but she didn't really want to contribute to the little girl's fear. "I won't, hon," Paige promised. "But if this is the kind of thing that's going to get them angry, then let's not do it again, okay? You can pretend all you want to, but if the other children don't want to play that way, then maybe it's just something you have to do on your own. Does that make sense? You wouldn't want Jonathan to cry again, would you?"

"No," Natalie said.

"Well, how about this," Paige asked, clapping her hands together in hopes of snapping Natalie out of her funk. "How about you draw a picture of your fairy for me?"

At this suggestion Natalie's eyes brightened. "Okay," she agreed, scampering over to the drawing table and selecting a giant sheet of pink construction paper. She settled at the table and grabbed at a thick purple crayon, barely pausing to look back at Paige.

Paige sighed. *That wasn't too hard,* she commended herself. She sneaked a peek at her watch: 12:02. Yikes. So much more time still to go. She'd need a serious caffeine boost if she was going to keep up with these kids.

"Crisis averted," came Katie's booming voice into Paige's ear. Paige was so startled she nearly jumped—she hadn't realized how much in her own mind she had been.

"Barely," Paige said, turning to face Katie. She grinned. "Jonathan would rather die than play with pretend fairies."

Katie smiled. "Children have such active imaginations," she mused.

Paige nodded. "Yup." *Never mind that fairies are, actually, totally real.*

Suddenly a thought occurred to Paige. Children could sometimes see fairies. Was it possible that Natalie's imagination wasn't entirely . . . imagined?

Or maybe Natalie was just a typical—though, it seemed, quite bright—four-year-old girl who still believed in enchanted princesses and knights, fairies and dragons. *All of which*, Paige reminded herself, *are completely real. But not many people know that.* In a few short years Natalie would almost definitely outgrow these beliefs. Better to just let her enjoy them for now. There was no reason to go making assumptions and starting trouble where, for once, there was no trouble to be found.

Right?

"What do you *mean* we don't have a band booked for the evening?" Piper demanded, leveling her part-time manager with a look of pure fury. "Garrett, it's a club. By its very definition there needs to be music. There's a band booked *every* evening."

"Sometimes there's a DJ," Garrett offered less than helpfully. He fixed Piper with a blank, blue-eyed stare.

Piper placed her hands on her hips. "Yes, sometimes. And yet tonight we have neither. Can you *please* explain to me how such a thing happens? And it better be good."

Today was Piper's second day back at P3 full-time, and it wasn't getting any easier. For starters, she was physically exhausted. Wyatt still wasn't sleeping straight through the night, which meant that Piper wasn't either. Leo was always game for helping out—even at two in the morning, God bless him—but it didn't matter: If Wyatt woke up, Piper woke up. So after a few failed attempts at getting a decent night's sleep, Piper told Leo not to even worry about it. She could take care of it. She could take care of it and *still* make it to P3 by ten every morning, ready to go another round.

Which might have worked out, actually, if things at P3 had managed to run smoothly. *But no, that would be too easy*, Piper thought grimly. She needed to talk to her accountant about getting her billing resolved. And somehow, inventory was way down. The champagne glasses had arrived yesterday—those that were intact, in any case—but that was about it. No other orders—except for more drink mixes—had been placed in the three months that Piper had been out. Meaning that the bar was dangerously low on pint glasses, tumblers, and plastic stirrers. *Not good*, Piper thought. She pressed her fingers against her temples and closed her eyes, willing the bad karma to just—*poof!*—clear up.

She opened her eyes. Garrett still stood in front of her. If anything, he looked more confused now than ever. "So, uh, what do you want me to do, Piper?" he asked, more than a little bit skittishly.

"Well, for starters, Garrett, you can explain to me how there is neither a band nor a DJ confirmed for this evening," Piper suggested, willing herself to stay calm. *Deep breaths. Deep, soothing breaths*, she thought.

Garrett squinted at her. "Do you have, like, asthma?" When Piper only glared back at him, he hurriedly continued, "Well, ah, the booking is all handled by Maria."

"Right," Piper said slowly, as if talking to an infant. "And?"

"Maria quit two weeks ago," Garrett said.

Piper sucked in all her breath at once. *To heck with deep and soothing*, she decided abruptly. "And you didn't think to tell me, or look into hiring a replacement for her, or—at the absolute very least—confirming the entertainment by yourself?"

Garrett looked like he was about to cry. "Those would have been good ideas," he admitted, thrusting his hands into the pockets of his jeans. "Good ideas," he repeated.

"Garrett?" Piper prompted, looking at him expectantly.

Garrett gazed at her, speechless.

"Why don't you try and confirm now?" she said quietly, on the verge of losing what very little cool she had left.

Garrett shifted his weight back and forth, looking incredibly uncomfortable. "It's just that, I, uh, have the rest of the night off," he said, refusing to meet her gaze.

"Of course you do," Piper agreed, for fear of saying anything more. "Why don't you run on home?"

As Garrett gratefully scampered out the door, Piper turned to survey the main room of the club once again. She had managed—with Garrett's help—to unload the boxes of glasses, to sweep, dust, and reorganize the bar area back to her liking. And she had sifted through most of the outstanding mail. Other than the music debacle—admittedly, not a small problem—things weren't exactly raging out of control. Sort of, but not *exactly*.

And yet.

Piper found that she just couldn't get Wyatt off her mind. This arrangement just wasn't going to work. The club needed someone's full-time attention. Someone at least marginally more responsible than Garrett, sure, but that someone was out there. And at the moment, at least, it wasn't Piper.

Piper reached into her jeans pocket and pulled out an elastic, fastening her long, thick hair into a low ponytail. She thrust her hands into the back pockets of her jeans and leaned heavily against the bar. She couldn't stand failing. And that's what this felt like. She didn't have the concentration and the energy to be Wyatt's mommy and P3's full-time manager. It was obvious that one or the other was going to suffer. And there was no way that she was going to let Wyatt be the one.

So much for doing it all, she thought glumly. *I can't even do it* some.

She looked at her watch: 5:00 PM. Paige would be on her way home with Wyatt right now. And where was she? In a club, surrounded by chaos, down one part-time manager and one DJ. And utterly frustrated. She couldn't go on this way. She needed to have more positive energy for her son, and for herself.

She was going to have to go back to being a full-time mommy. That was the only answer. Otherwise the guilt—and the double life—was going to kill her.

I start tomorrow, she said to herself. *Tonight, after all, I've got to figure out the DJ mess, talk to Maria about her resignation, and get in touch with a manager I can trust while I'm home.*

It'll only be another month or two, Piper promised herself. *Then I can go back to being superwoman. For right now, I'll settle for being supermom.*

Starting tomorrow.

With fixed determination Piper headed back toward her office—and her Rolodex. She had a few phone calls she needed to make.

Across town, over at the *Bay Mirror* offices, Phoebe was having a late night herself. She was buried in a pile of increasingly frantic letters from nervous new mothers. *I don't get it,* she thought to herself. There was nothing to account for what felt like an enormous baby boom in the last few months.

> *Dear Phoebe—*
>
> *My husband and I have been married for a little more than three years now, and the whole time I've known him he's been incredibly considerate and thoughtful. That is, until last month, when I gave birth to our first child.*
>
> *Suddenly the man who wouldn't leave the house without asking me if I needed anything never thinks to ask what I might need now (an extra hour of sleep, an extra pair of hands around the house . . .)! And while he never used to be one for going out "with the boys," these days it's happening more and more often. I could really use more help from him, but I*

don't know how to ask. Anything I can think of saying sounds like whining. Any advice?
—Desperate

Phoebe pushed herself back in her chair and cracked her knuckles. The only advice she could think of for Desperate was to tell her husband where to get off, and she didn't really expect that would be especially productive. Besides, she knew that newborn babies put a strain on even the most ideal relationships. Heck, Piper and Leo had had their share of difficulties. Desperate needed real advice, advice that suddenly, Phoebe was fresh out of. Who even knew? Maybe Desperate's husband was as freaked out by the new baby as she was, and that was why he was suddenly channeling his inner jerk. That was possible, wasn't it?

"Elise!" Phoebe called out, somewhat desperate herself as she caught sight of her boss passing the doorway to her office.

Elise doubled back and poked her head into Phoebe's office. "Yes?"

"Okay, so let's say your husband's this awesome guy, right?"

Elise shot Phoebe a look. "In what imaginary world is this imaginary husband so fantastic? 'Cause I'd like to visit," she quipped.

"Work with me," Phoebe insisted. "And then you've got your first baby, and it's up all night crying, puking, making messes in its diapers.

And you're both tired and weirded out, and all of the baby books are, like, contradicting one another. I mean, would that be a recipe for an invasion of the husband snatchers? Under those circumstances, I mean, someone normal might start being less like himself, right?" She peered at her boss expectantly over the rims of her glasses.

Elise burst out laughing. "Is Piper's husband refusing diaper duty?" she asked, hugely amused. "Phoebe—it'll pass. He's just being a *guy*," she said, her voice dripping with scorn. "But really," she continued, gesturing at the pile of letters spilling out from Phoebe's in-box, "don't you have enough to do of your own, rather than to get overinvested in your sister's child rearing? Honestly, Phoebe," Elise said, sounding disappointed, "I thought Jason had talked to you about this."

"No, it's not Pi—," Phoebe began to call out. She stopped abruptly. It was no use. Elise was already gone, disappeared down the hall.

Phoebe slumped over her desk, chin in hand. What was going on with her? She was normally so good at what she did! But suddenly it felt like the whole world had a problem that she just couldn't solve. Usually, when it came to giving advice, Phoebe could just go with her gut. But lately, that gut instinct was plain out to lunch.

And "Ask Phoebe" was fresh out of ideas.

Chapter Three

"I thought you'd be supportive of this," Piper said, frowning at her husband. "Given how concerned you were when I went back to work in the first place."

She reached for the jug of milk to pour some in her morning coffee. She didn't understand Leo's behavior one bit. By the time she'd gotten home the night before, he had been fast asleep, so she hadn't had the chance to fill him in on her decision regarding staying home with Wyatt. She'd outlined the sketchy details when they both woke up for Wyatt's 5:00 AM feeding. He had been less than thrilled with the idea, surprisingly. *Okay, so maybe not the best time to drop important news*, Piper admitted to herself, sweeping her hair out of her face and taking a hearty swig from her coffee mug, *but still.* "Weren't you the one who thought I was taking on too much too soon?" she pointed out.

Leo sighed and leveled a steady gaze at Piper from across the kitchen table. "Yes, I was," he agreed. "I thought it was unrealistic of you to think that you would be able to work and be Mom—*and* live up to your own high standards—so quickly after giving birth. And I still think that my concerns hold true."

"So then, you should be thrilled that I've decided to quit the club for now," Piper insisted. "No more biting off more than I can chew! It's the best possible scenario. For the time being, that is," she was quick to add. "I spent all last night on the phone looking for staff to cover my leave. The club is in good hands. Better hands than my own! I've been too distracted, thinking about Wyatt and wondering how he's doing all day. But that's all solved now. And Wyatt will be in the best hands! His *mother's*," she said with emphasis, as if Leo needed any clarification. "Where's the downside?"

"No downside," Leo agreed. "I'm not worried about the club, and I'm definitely not worried about Wyatt."

"Well then, that'd just leave me," Piper said, with a level gaze on Leo. She drummed her fingers on the kitchen tabletop.

"Yes. To be frank? I'm worried about you," Leo stated with finality. He paused to gauge Piper's reaction.

She squinted at him. "In what way? You were right—trying to do both was making me a mad-

woman. So for now, I'll be Mommie Dearest.
Except, you know—*really* Mommie Dearest. Not
in a scary way," she explained.

"The thing is, Piper," Leo began gently,
"you're the most driven, dynamic woman I've
ever known. Since I've met you, you've gone
from being a shy, insecure middle sister to a successful businesswoman, the heart of this family,
and a protector of Innocents who never shirks
her responsibilities—Charmed or otherwise.
You're amazing," he said softly, reaching across
the table to take her hand. "Completely unlike
anyone I've known. And entirely prone to taking
on the entire world at a time."

Piper stared at him. She was touched, but she
didn't quite get what he was saying.

"It's always all or nothing with you," he finished. "After Prue died, you took up the mantle,
and you haven't eased up once."

"I *can't* ease up," Piper protested. "Every day
there's something new out there to fight against."

"I understand that, Piper," Leo said. "The
point is that with you, there's no such thing as
compromise. Once Wyatt was old enough to be
left on his own for a few hours a day, you were
determined to be *uber*-Piper, Mom of the Year by
day, savvy club owner by night, and Charmed
One . . . well, all the time. There was no room for
you to breathe. No way to ease in to things."

"I'm not so much of an ease-er," Piper confessed. It was the truth.

"I know," Leo said, nodding. "That's one of the things I love most about you. But if you want to be a mother to Wyatt, a sister to Paige and Phoebe, a manager at P3, *and* a Charmed One, you might have to learn how to scale back a little bit. If you give one hundred percent to each of those . . . Well, the math just doesn't add up."

Piper rested her chin in her hand thoughtfully. "You have a point," she said. "So I'm not sure why you're not more enthusiastic about me slowing down."

"I think it's a great idea for you to slow down," Leo said. "Don't get me wrong. But I don't want you to always think of everything in such 'either-or' terms. You were distracted at the club, so now you're going to stay home with Wyatt indefinitely. You have this idea that it's always choice A or choice B—and maybe in this case, it is. Maybe. I guess only time will tell. But it's not always so cut-and-dried, you know."

Piper nodded. "I hear you. But this is the *right* choice for me right now." She took a sip of her coffee and leaned back, feeling the most relaxed she'd been all week. At the heart of Leo's argument was only love and concern. She considered herself very fortunate to have someone like him in her life. Especially after all they'd been through together.

"I respect your choice," Leo assured her. "You know yourself. Just don't push yourself too hard . . . in *any* direction." He stood up and walked around the table to where Piper sat and began to rub her shoulders.

"Remind me again how I got so lucky to have an angel—literally—for my husband?" Piper asked teasingly. She closed her eyes and allowed herself to enjoy a brief moment of privacy with Leo. Any minute now Paige and Phoebe would be stumbling out of bed to go to work—or Wyatt would wake once again—and the spell would be broken.

Leo leaned forward and kissed her on the tip of her nose playfully. "Magic."

He orbed off in a shower of white light, leaving Piper to begin her day at home with Wyatt in earnest.

Thank goodness I decided to stay home with Wyatt when I did, Piper thought that afternoon. *Another week at the day care center and I wouldn't know my own son anymore.*

Okay, so maybe it was a *slight* bit of exaggeration, but the truth was, that as the day wore on, Piper couldn't shake the feeling that Wyatt just wasn't being himself. It was totally paranoid, she knew, to assume that something was wrong, or that he could have changed so drastically in a span of only a few days. She'd certainly been touchy enough lately—but could her maternal instinct really, truly be so off?

She glanced down at Wyatt's stroller as he scrunched his tiny face together, looking for all the world as though he was preparing to let loose with an earth-shattering wail. Which he probably was. Her normally even-tempered child had apparently taken to bursting into hysterical tears every ten seconds or so since his days with Paige at the day care center. It was worrisome, but more than that, it was actually getting kind of embarrassing.

Piper hadn't thought much of it when they were at the cleaners' earlier that morning. After all, what infant didn't humiliate his or her parents with an ill-timed shriek now and again. But when it happened at the butcher's, the mechanic's, and finally, when she stopped for a coffee, she had to wonder. After all, his feedings had been on time—hadn't they?

Yes, she remembered, absently pushing Wyatt down the "hair care" aisle of the drugtore, *but then again, he didn't have his usual appetite. He refused at least half of each bottle, and spit up a decent amount of what he did eat.* Again, not unheard of for babies, but fairly unusual for Wyatt.

Piper tossed a bottle of shampoo into the basket she was carrying and rounded a corner sharply. Her jeans caught under the wheels of the stroller, stopping her short. She looked down to check for rips, but luckily, everything was where it should be. She started down the next aisle and grabbed a package of Q-Tips and some shaving cream for Leo, then made her way toward the front of the store to get on line. Just when she was allowing herself the hope that perhaps she and Wyatt were actually going to make it out of the drugstore without a crying fit, he opened his mouth and squealed like he'd seen a ghost.

Piper had seen plenty of evil during her time saving Innocents as a Charmed One, but her spider-sense told her instantly that there was no demonic activity going on in the store, save for a painfully slow sixteen-year-old girl behind the counter. And even that was only figurative evil. So it was safe to assume that Wyatt was merely having a temper tantrum.

An impossibly loud temper tantrum.

"Oh, it's okay, Wyatt, Mommy's here," Piper cooed, setting down her basket to wave a plastic rattle in front of his face. But if anything, Wyatt's screams grew louder and more urgent.

"Oh, hey, baby, what's the matter?" Piper sang, taking Wyatt out of the stroller and bouncing him on her hip in a last-ditch effort to soothe him. No dice. He wrapped his fist around a thick clump of her hair and tugged. Hard. Piper had to struggle not to react, since that clearly wasn't going to do anything to diffuse the situation. She had to somehow calm him down. Not to mention, people were starting to stare.

"Maybe he's colicky," offered a heavyset woman whose face was framed with tight, reddish blond ringlets. She pursed her pink-lacquered lips together in a fake smile that suggested grave doubts about Piper's parenting skills.

Piper resisted the urge to tell pink-lips where to get off, instead offering only her own tight, tired grin. "Who knows?" she said as lightly as she could. She squeaked out a small chuckle that fell flat as it hit the air.

"Well, you oughta be careful about that," pink-lips continued, clearly completely unaware that she was treading on dangerously thin ice. "It can get worse before it gets better." She folded her arms authoritatively across her ample chest.

"And you sure wouldn't want *that* to get worse." This bit of unsolicited and unwelcome advice came from an elderly woman, also in line, so skinny she looked as though she might crack in half at the slightest hint of a breeze. There was no mistaking her feelings about Wyatt's crying.

"Well, you know, babies cry," Piper said, feeling uncharacteristically flustered. *But not* mine! she thought wildly. Before she and Leo had agreed that they were ready for children, they'd once found themselves in a store filled with screaming babies . . . and the thought of it still sent shivers down her spine. After Wyatt was born, she'd thought of herself as lucky: Her baby didn't have shrieking fits. Ever.

Though of course this little incident—along with a dozen others that afternoon—suggested otherwise. Piper let the awkward teenager ring up her purchases—moving so slowly it was as though the girl was working underwater—

slapped her money down on the counter, snatched up her change, and fled the store, her cheeks flaming in embarrassment. Anyone watching the scene would think she was a kidnapper, the way Wyatt was carrying on.

What was going on with him?

"Honey, I'm home!" Paige called energetically, stepping through the doorway of the Manor.

"Oh, no, wait, don't—," Piper shouted, jumping up from the living-room couch and deftly leaping into the foyer in no more than three great strides.

"Don't what?" Paige asked, puzzled, pushing the door shut behind her. It bounced into place with a loud bang.

"—slam the door," Piper finished wearily. She paused, held herself very still, and cocked her head at an angle. No noise from Wyatt's nursery. Meaning, the front door closing hadn't woken him up. *Thank goodness*, she thought wryly. *Small favors and all that.*

She had *just* gotten Wyatt down for a nap—his first for the day—moments before Paige had arrived. And after the day that the two of them had had, she really thought he needed it. Or maybe she was the one who needed it. Either way, it had come, at last, and she wasn't fool enough to look a gift horse in the mouth.

"Never mind," she said, straightening up and dusting off the front of her jeans. "He didn't wake up, and therefore, I don't have to kill you."

"Well, hello to you, too, Sis," Paige said, setting her bag down next to her house keys on the small table in the hallway. "I guess I don't have to ask how your day was."

"Oh, you don't even want to know how my day was. I can't bear to replay it for you. I am totally and completely wiped. I hope you don't mind takeout for dinner," Piper said.

"I thought you were going to go all 1950s housewife on us, now that you're home with Wyatt all day. Major disappointment," Paige said slyly. "*Kidding*," she added hastily, seeing the look on Piper's face. "Why don't you take a load off? Have a seat in the living room and I'll bring in some tea. We can both kick back. Chamomile?"

"Mmmm. Perfect. You're a saint," Piper agreed. She grabbed a glossy clothing catalog from the stack of mail sitting on the front table and headed for the sofa. "I'll just be here getting a head start on the relaxation."

Once the tea was ready, Paige joined her sister in the living room. Piper had already gone to work marking her favorite catalog selections. "Don't you love these pants? And this tank—that'd be a great color for you," Piper suggested, holding the book out to Paige.

Paige leaned forward and peered at the image. "True. Hey, it's almost the same color as *that*," she said, pointing at a crusty stain on the sleeve of Piper's shirt. She wrinkled her nose. "What is that, anyway?"

Piper glanced down at her sleeve and shrugged. "I have no idea. And I'm too tired to think about it."

Paige frowned at Piper sympathetically. "So I take it Wyatt wasn't being 'happy baby' today?"

"Wyatt was being *Invasion of the Body Snatchers* baby today. Seriously, Paige, he was like an alien, like something possessed. I mean, I guess all babies have their days now and then, but Wyatt was *not* himself. Not once, from morning to night. He was like a demon child or something."

Paige looked at her sister quizzically. "Okay, call me paranoid witchy, but you *are* being metaphorical, right? I mean, you don't really think that the boy is possessed by evil things? Because that would be bad."

"Uh, you think so?" Piper asked. "That would be way more than bad, Paige. But no, I guess it seems like normal baby bad news, not evil of the serious variety."

"Serious evil? Say more!"

Piper and Paige had been so engrossed in their conversation that they hadn't even heard Phoebe come in, home from work at last. "Wait, don't—," Piper began, starting to put down her teacup.

The door slammed shut.

"Never mind," Piper finished, defeated.

"Wyatt is napping," Paige said, tilting her

head toward the front stairs. "Shhh!" She held her forefinger to her lips exaggeratedly. Phoebe looked crestfallen.

"Oh, it's fine. You didn't wake him up. Sit. Have tea," Piper said, patting the couch next to her. "Tell us about your day. We can compare notes. And horror stories."

"Ugh, horror stories," Phoebe said, taking off her jacket and hanging it in the front closet. She crossed into the living room and collapsed into a chair, her legs thrust out in front of her like a five-year-old in time-out. "I am having *such* writer's bl—" She broke off when she saw the dark circles under Piper's eyes. "Do you want to go first?" she asked gently.

"I don't know what it is, Phoebes," Piper confessed. "I wanted to stay home with Wyatt—heck, I even thought I *had* to, the job I was doing at the club—but let me tell you, it hasn't exactly been fun and games today. My beautiful baby boy is a total holy terror."

"And you're thinking serious evil?" Phoebe guessed, picking up on the conversation where she had walked in. "Not just cranky baby?"

Piper looked thoughtful. "Well, okay, cranky baby is definitely a viable option. And probably should be considered our top choice. But I have to wonder if something else isn't going on. I mean, Wyatt just isn't being himself. He's not eating, he's not sleeping, he's been crying *all* day—"

"He puked a few times too," Paige added helpfully, pointing at the stain on Piper's sleeve for good measure.

"I mean, that's not my boy," Piper said finally, sighing and leaning back against the sofa. "He's had a complete personality transplant—overnight!" She turned to Paige. "Tell me honestly, Paige—was he like this at the center?"

Paige shook her head no, looking earnest. "I swear, he was completely his normal self," she promised.

"Well, wait a minute, before we go totally freaking out," Phoebe interjected. "I mean, he's only a few months old. During their first year, babies develop at an amazing rate."

"You've been keeping up with your baby books," Paige noted, impressed.

Phoebe nodded, feeling self-conscious about the extra research she'd been doing. "I know you think he isn't being himself, Piper, and I want to give you the benefit of the doubt, but isn't it possible that at this age, he doesn't really have a 'self' just yet?" She turned to face her sister, looking sincere.

Piper pursed her lips. "You make a good point," she conceded.

"Sometimes a mother knows," Paige offered, feeling a bit like a referee at a tennis match.

"Yeah . . . ," Phoebe said, allowing her words to trail off. Her agreement sounded hollow, even to her own ears. She knew she was right. After all, she'd read three different baby books on her lunch break this afternoon. Or, at least, she'd skimmed their respective tables of contents. But then again . . . she *still* hadn't finished her column, had she? She was still avoiding all of the eager new mothers. For some reason she suddenly doubted her own capacity to give advice. Maybe that meant it was time to take a step back from playing "Ask Phoebe" at home, too? "Yeah, you're probably right," she finished finally, dubious.

A shower of lights from the direction of the kitchen caught the girls' attention and effectively put an end to any further conversation.

"Thank goodness Leo can orb," Paige commented. "At least you know he's not going to slam any doors and—"

She was abruptly cut off by the sound of a plate hitting the tiled floor and shattering into pieces.

"Sorry!" Leo called cheerfully.

From upstairs, Wyatt began to wail mournfully.

"Never mind," Piper grumbled, pushing herself up from the couch with a heavy sigh. "I'll take care of it."

Chapter Four

"It's just you and me in our group today, dear," Dori said as Paige arrived at the day care center Friday morning—almost half an hour late, which was quickly becoming her habit. "I hope you've had your coffee. You're going to need it."

Paige took off her denim jacket and hung it in the coat closet in the small back office, dropping her bag behind the door as well. She smoothed her capris and T-shirt (both in dark colors to hide grimy kid spills) and walked back out into the main room.

Dori's warning was true. A small army of hellions was racing around the floor, and Katie was nowhere to be seen. Paige wrapped her hair into a ponytail and crossed to the small kitchenette. Thankfully Dori had already started a pot of coffee. She poured herself a mug and dumped in a healthy spoonful of sugar. *Nothing wrong with a sugar rush*, she thought, stirring the contents of the mug energetically and taking a hearty gulp.

Dori walked in behind her and poured herself a cup. "Where's Katie? Out sick?" Paige asked. "I hope she didn't catch whatever Simon was peddling," she added, flashing back to a small puking incident from the previous afternoon. *Come to think of it, where's Simon?* she thought, casting a sharp eye toward the bassinets in the nursery. The nurse on infant duty was bustling around, but Simon was nowhere in sight.

Dori shrugged, looking perplexed. "It was the strangest thing. She didn't necessarily say that she was sick. For that matter, she didn't really say anything conclusive at all. She just left a message saying that she wouldn't be coming in to work anymore."

"Ever?" Paige asked, surprised. She cocked an eyebrow in disbelief. "As in, never again?"

Dori shook her head. "It looks that way."

"Well, what does that mean for us? Other than you and me putting in more effort today, I guess. I mean, long term," Paige said, feeling slightly panicked. The center felt plenty busy even when all three of them were on duty! How would they manage being short staffed?

"I'll have to call the employment agency that sent her, of course. This is highly unprofessional," Dori said. "To tell you the truth, I was completely blindsided. Katie had such a knack with the kids. She was a natural. Not to mention, to quit without any notice is just so *terribly* unprofessional," she repeated. She glared at Paige accusatorily.

"Oh, well, I know!" Paige agreed enthusiastically. She didn't want to condemn Katie without hearing her side of the story, but she wasn't about to tell Dori that. Paige checked her watch. It was 8:45 AM, which was the official start of the day at the center. Normally Dori and the other group leaders arrived at 8:00 to open and set up. Paige and Katie and the rest of the assistants would come in between 8:15 and 8:30, so that they could be there when the children started to filter in. Most of the children at the center had parents who worked full-time, hence the need for day care. For that reason, by 8:45 nearly all the children had been dropped off.

And yet Simon was nowhere to be seen. Sure, some of the kids had parents who worked part-time, or who made alternate arrangements on certain days, but Paige had made it a point early on Monday morning to look over everyone's schedule and familiarize herself with the regulars. Simon, she knew, was a regular. "Dori—what about Simon? Is *he* out sick? Or did something else come up?"

Dori looked uncomfortable. She glanced away and fiddled at the hem of her blouse. "Well, now, his mother called me this morning," she began nervously. "Simon's not coming back either."

"Huh?" Paige asked. "Why not?" Simon had been a perfectly placid seven-month-old. He liked to sit on the floor and play with big, plastic blocks. Nothing ever fazed him, except on the rare occasion that another child tried to share the blocks—Simon wasn't so into sharing. But the other kids learned that quickly. In addition to the fact that she'd miss him and his easy laughter, it just seemed odd that he would be whisked out without good reason. He had been so happy at the center, after all. And his mother was a news reporter who worked long hours. What were the odds that she suddenly wasn't working anymore?

Dori gave Paige a meaningful look and took her lightly by the elbow, leading her to the farthest corner of the main room, where they could keep an eye on their charges but also speak freely without worrying that the kids would hear them. "It was just so strange, I tell you," she said, once they were safely out of earshot. "She called just furious. She told me that Simon wasn't being his normal self. He was being fussier than usual, crying all the time, refusing to eat, sulking, avoiding his favorite toys . . . just being terrible, she says. Very unlike his typical demeanor. And she blames us."

A cold shiver pricked down Paige's spine. *Not being his normal 'self,'* she thought, remembering her sisters' conversation the night before. Wyatt was being weird too, according to Piper. And as much as Phoebe had made a persuasive "don't worry your pretty little head" argument, suddenly Paige had to wonder. Was there something about the center? Something that was causing drastic changes in temperament among its charges? Suddenly that theory sounded a lot more plausible. But what, really, could be affecting the babies? Separation anxiety? Or something more sinister?

"You know, my sister was mentioning that Wyatt was being a little crabby at home yesterday," Paige commented, aiming for casual and missing it by at least a yard. "I wonder if they both had . . . something," she finished, knowing as she said it that there really wasn't much both babies could have "had." A bug? A bug bite? An "off" bottle? Or maybe they'd just eaten something linty off the floor when everyone's backs were turned?

"Oh, you know," Dori said offhandedly, "Wyatt hadn't even been here a week. Babies take some time to adjust to day care. For that matter, all kids do. I can't worry too much about it. It's just the one isolated incident."

Well, except, it's sort of two, Paige thought, but she held her tongue. If something was going on, she'd be better able to get to the bottom of it.

"What about Katie, though?"

"What *about* her?" Dori asked, sounding startled and somewhat impatient. "I told you— it was very inappropriate for her to leave so abruptly, and I won't be giving her a reference, I can assure you of that. But what would that have to do with one seven-month-old being pulled out by his mother?"

Paige was unconvinced. "Maybe Katie couldn't handle the fact that the kids were all developing bad attitudes? Maybe she was fed up?"

"If she was 'fed up,' as you say, with babies and young children having an off day, then she certainly is in the wrong business!" Dori said loudly. Looking around at the children, she lowered her voice to add, "Although, come to think of it, I suppose technically at this point she's no longer *in* the business. Which is probably just as well."

Paige toyed with the handle of her coffee cup, on the verge of protesting. But Dori clearly didn't want to discuss the matter any further.

"Paige, why don't you get all of our fours and fives on the story mat for morning meeting," she suggested quietly but firmly. "I'm going to gather the twos and threes."

Paige opened her mouth to respond, thought better of it, and walked back to the center of the room. She clapped her hands together overhead. "Come on, Dori's group!" she called. "Fours and fives, it's time for MORNING MEETING!" She was overcompensating for feeling tired and unmotivated, she knew, but it seemed to work.

Instantly the children in her group dropped their playthings and made a beeline to the story mat. The story mat was actually just a threadbare circular rug in the center of the main room, but the kids loved it. Sitting on the story mat meant one of two things: one, that they were about to be read a story, which always seemed to go over well. Or two, that it was time for morning meeting, where different children got to stand up and deliver little speeches about the date, time, weather, and what was on the "agenda" for the day. It was also when "Kid of the Day" was announced. Morning meeting was the time of the day when Paige most had the children's attention, so she was happy to be turning toward it now, even though she was still feeling pretty unsatisfied from her conversation with Dori.

After all the kids were sitting on the mat, Paige placed her hand on the head of a little boy. "Dylan, you're the Kid of the Day!" she said.

"Today is Friday," stammered Dylan. His watery blue eyes were wide with the total shock of being named Kid of the Day. Paige was about to hand him his special badge when the phone rang.

"One sec, Dylan—" Paige said, holding her hand out. But when she turned to head off in the direction of the phone, she saw that Dori had already grabbed it.

"Oh, *hello*," Dori said into the receiver, sounding suddenly very alert. Paige stiffened.

"Today is *Friday*," Dylan continued insistently, reaching for his badge. Paige intercepted his chubby fist with her own and knelt down to face him. "Shhh, just for a moment," she said, putting her index finger to her lips. "Just until Dori's off the phone, okay? We want her to be able to hear." She straightened herself up and ruffled his thick, sandy hair. *And we want to be able to hear Dori,* she thought. The expression on Dori's face did not look good, no doubt about it.

"I see," Dori was saying into the phone. "I see, yes. So not today, then. Right." Pause. "And not next week." Pause again. "Oh, so—then not ever . . . again . . . is what you're saying. I see." A slightly longer pause, fraught with awkward tension. "And may I ask why not? No, just for our own knowledge, of course. Customer satisfaction and the like . . . Oh. *Oh.* I see. How unusual. No, certainly that's the first we've heard of anything at all like that."

Like what? Paige wondered feverishly. But she bet she could guess.

"Well, then, thanks so much for calling, and I'm very sorry to hear the news. Do let us know if you change your mind," Dori said. She pursed her lips into a thin line and slowly, deliberately placed the telephone back onto its base.

"Can I go *now*?" Dylan asked, the instant Dori had hung up the phone. Paige nearly jumped out of her skin. She'd been so focused on Dori's conversation that she had almost forgotten about Dylan entirely. *Speaking of unprofessional,* she thought wildly.

"Well, sweetie, I need to go talk to Dori," Paige said. She handed him his badge. "This is your badge—because you're the Kid of the Day!" she said, smiling winningly. "Now, as your first official Kid of the Day duty, why don't you hand out the construction paper and crayons, and everyone can draw for a little while? We can go over the agenda a little bit later. Sound good?"

A resounding chorus of "YEAH" flew back at Paige. Drawing was always a big hit. Everyone scrambled for their assigned seats at the worktables that were arranged in a semicircle around the story mat, while Dylan collected the art supplies, looking extremely pleased with himself. Paige grinned at him encouragingly, then joined Dori over by the phone.

"Who was that?" she asked, crossing her arms expectantly across her chest.

"Betsey's mother," Dori said, exhaling loudly. Betsey was another infant who had been in Dori's group.

"And?" Paige pressed.

"Betsey's been very irritable these past few days, and her parents wonder if she wouldn't do better to spend a little more time with them at home," Dori said. She said the words in such a way that Paige knew she was quoting verbatim. "Paige, I don't think we need to overreact. This is a day care center, not a boarding school. Children do come and go as their parents see fit. Usually it's to their own advantage. Besides, we don't know that this is permanent."

Except that I heard you on the phone, Paige thought. *You said it yourself—it is permanent! She's not coming back—not ever!*

"I noticed you cut morning meeting short," Dori said disapprovingly. "You might want to go back to the main area and supervise them while they color." She turned on her heel and marched back toward the group of younger children, leaving Paige with the distinct impression that she was not exactly on her boss's good side. *Great,* she thought.

Oh, well. Nothing to do about it now.

She did a quick lap around the children's tables, leaning in to see their artwork. Dylan had, predictably, drawn a portrait of himself as Kid of the Day. The badge figured prominently in his illustration. Natalie had drawn a typical nuclear family standing outside a house. It was the same drawing that lots of the children did, offering up variations that corresponded to their own families and their own lives. Natalie had added a personal touch, of course—in the form of a small, Tinkerbell-esque fairy hovering just above the chimney. Paige caught Natalie's eye as she passed and smiled encouragingly.

Luckily Jonathan was nowhere nearby, so

Natalie was free to imagine to her heart's content. And Paige was free to puzzle over the disturbing trend among the infants. . . .

"Okay, riddle me this, 'Ask Phoebe,'" Paige said to her sister that night over dinner. "At what age, exactly, *do* infants start to develop a personality?"

"Why are you asking that now?" Piper asked suspiciously. "You seemed pretty noncommittal when we talked about it the other night."

The sisters—plus Leo—were gathered around the dining-room table for the first sit-down meal they'd had all week. Leo had come home early enough in the day that Piper was able to steal away to the market to buy groceries for dinner. She hadn't had the energy to make anything fancy, but the small effort went a long way toward making everyone feel human at the end of a long workweek. Now, halfway through dinner, a vegetable lasagna—minus many helpings—sat in the center of the table next to a huge bowl of fresh salad. Leo had even opened a bottle of wine. "It's Friday night," he'd explained, feeling festive.

Piper leaned forward and picked at a stray piece of cheese from the pasta on her plate. "I thought you were on Phoebe's side before. I thought I was overreacting," she continued.

Paige raised an eyebrow and held up a hand in protest. "I'm not on anyone's side!" she said, taking a sip of water. "No sides. Well, maybe Wyatt's. Phoebe made a pretty strong argument is all I was saying. But some stuff happened today at the center that made me sort of rethink it all."

"What happened?" Leo asked, sounding concerned. "Is everyone okay?"

"Yes, definitely—I think," Paige said. "It was weird. Two different mothers decided not to bring their kids back today. Like, just dropped out, without any real explanation."

"Doesn't that ever happen?" Phoebe asked. "I mean, maybe the parents switched their work hours or something? It could happen."

"Yeah, true, but both of these mothers took the time to call up the center and actually complain."

"Complain about what?" Piper asked.

"That their babies were acting . . . weird," Paige admitted.

"Weird like how?" Piper asked slowly.

Paige could see the wheels turning in her sister's head as they had in her own that morning. "Honestly? Weird like Wyatt," she admitted. "Grouchy, cranky, restless . . . won't go down for naps, won't eat . . . Just total personality transplants."

"I told you," Phoebe began, sighing, "this is totally—"

"Yeah, yeah, totally normal, and babies don't have personalities yet, etcetera, etcetera," Paige said. "And, like I said, yesterday I was on your side."

"I thought you said you weren't on any sides," Piper pointed out.

Paige sighed in frustration. "*So* not the issue!" she said defensively. "Work with me, people. Yesterday I thought Phoebe made sense. But today, the two babies who were pulled were very sweet, even-tempered infants. I mean, these kids *never* fussed or cried. It's strange. The only thing I can think that makes sense is that maybe day care is just having a bad effect."

"I don't buy it," Piper interjected. "You know I was trying not to jump to conclusions—still am, in fact—but how can day care be evil? I mean, I did my homework. You know me. I would never have sent Wyatt to day care if it weren't for the fact that it's known to be totally fine for kids, developmentally speaking. So why would it be messing with the moods of infants unless it was something more specific?"

"Like what?" Leo asked. "Don't you think if something were going on—*really* going on, I mean—that the Elders would have clued me in?" He stood and started to clear the plates from dinner, stacking them in his arms and carrying them into the kitchen.

"I didn't say I was sure it was magic related," Paige said. "All I know for now is that it's weird. And that what started as a personal thing— Wyatt's behavior—may be connected to something larger. You know, one of the nurses quit today without notice."

"But again—maybe she quit because the kids were being bratty, and she couldn't take it," Phoebe suggested.

Paige shot a look across the table to her sister. "It just seems like a huge coincidence," she mused, leaning her chin in her hand in concentration.

"I'm not trying to ignore your concerns, Paige," Phoebe said, running her fingers through her hair. "But you have to admit that everything you're mentioning, frankly, *can* be explained away in non-Charmed terms. Right?"

Paige looked away. "Yeah?" she replied doubtfully. "Then how come Piper and I can't shake the idea that something is wrong?"

"Girls," Leo said, coming back into the room with a dish towel to wipe down the table. "I think Paige just hit the nail on the head. It's simple: Paige is concerned. And yesterday Piper was concerned. And if there's one thing we've all learned fighting evil together, it's that we can't ignore our inner warning bells. So let's not be so quick to ignore what might be going on here," he said authoritatively.

Phoebe cocked an eyebrow at him, unconvinced.

"*Might* be going on," he repeated. "That's all I'm saying."

"Aye-aye," Piper said, mock-saluting him.

"Well, what does that mean for me? I have *no* leads," Paige reminded everyone.

"Why don't you try to track down Katie? Try to find out where she is, why she quit," Leo replied. "That's a start."

"You're right. And it's something I can do before Monday," Paige said. "Instead of sitting around worrying."

"There's something else you can do," Piper suggested. "It would mean a lot to me."

"Sure, anything," Paige said automatically. "What is it?"

"Dessert," Piper quipped. "It's in the kitchen. Sorbet and fruit salad. Why don't you be a dear and bring it out to us," she said, winking devilishly.

Paige sighed heavily in mock frustration and hoisted herself out of her chair. "As usual, pick on the youngest," she complained, padding into the kitchen smiling good-naturedly.

"Been there, done that, your turn!" Phoebe called after her. "Don't forget spoons!"

Chapter Five

Oh, Internet, how thou hast forsaken me, Paige thought forlornly. She glanced to her right and to her left. On either side of her, people were hunched over computer keyboards, tapping away, oblivious to her fruitless online searches.

Joe's Java was the coolest place in town to get wired, literally and figuratively. The small-scale shop offered the best cup of coffee around, and Paige's fellow Bay Area residents much preferred it to certain larger corporate chains. The place was furnished in comfortable castoff chic, and no one minded if you came and camped out for the afternoon. The recent addition of a few Internet hookups only made Joe's more popular.

It was Saturday morning, and Paige had awoken at the first sign of sunlight with the nagging doubts about Katie and the day care center already gnawing away at her. She'd tossed and turned for a while, but ultimately decided to give up and dive into the day. She wasn't doing anyone any good lying in bed stressing.

It turned out that she hadn't been the only early riser. Phoebe had taken her laptop off to the park to work on her column, leaving Paige with no Internet access. She didn't mind, though, coming to Joe's. The clientele was young and hip, and the place had a vibe that managed to mellow her out and energize her all at once. For example, the couple reclining in the loveseat in the window could not have looked more relaxed—heads back, bodies intertwined, facing each other, hands laced together—but at the same time, they looked to be deep in a pretty intense conversation. She could think of worse places to kill an afternoon.

Which was what it looked like she was going to be doing. Because all of her detective work was turning up a big, fat zero.

She'd done a preliminary search online for Katie's address and phone number, planning to stop by for a visit and a polite chat later that afternoon. But Katie wasn't listed. At all. She wasn't even listed as "unlisted," which was bizarre. It was as though there wasn't even any trace of her.

Of course, there was the possibility that Katie lived with a boyfriend, friend, or other room-mate who had ordered the phone service in his or her own name. That would explain the lack of known address and phone number. All in all, the absence of a white-pages listing wasn't incriminating in itself.

So Paige had moved on.

When her "Katie Whitesmith" search had turned up a big, honking lack of results, Paige began to get suspicious. *Everyone* had at least one hit somewhere. Right?

She tried an experiment and typed in Phoebe's name. Big mistake. Every byline Phoebe'd ever had leaped off the screen. Hundreds of hits. Paige's head spun. She cleared the search box and tried again. "Piper Halliwell." Again, two full pages of hits, mostly reviews—favorable reviews—of P3. *I'll have to tell her about that*, Paige thought to herself. Especially since Piper had been so paranoid lately about the club going downhill now that she was a full-time mama.

Focus, Paige, focus, she reminded herself, shaking her head and facing the screen again. *Okay, well, I'm not in the media the way that my sisters are. So I should try me. I mean, it would just sort of prove my point.*

"Paige Matthews."

It was nothing like the search she'd done for Phoebe, though of course that made sense. And yet, here were two articles that made mention of her. One was the Web site of the social work agency she'd been with when she first met her half sisters. She was listed as one of their "newest and brightest." *Also good to know*, she thought to herself, feeling a flash of pride. Discovering she was a witch-Whitelighter had taken its toll on her career, and it was nice to know that she *had* been appreciated, at one point or another, even if she ultimately had to leave the agency behind.

The other was a picture of her from an article about Piper and P3. It was one of the same hits she'd gotten when she had searched for Piper's name.

Okay, so maybe I'm not taking the online world by storm, but there you have it—everyone has at least one hit online, she thought to herself, feeling vindicated. Then it occurred to her that once again she was fresh out of leads on Katie. She sighed deeply.

"Hey, that didn't sound good," said her next-door neighbor, a sandy blond guy with deep brown eyes and a quizzical smile.

Paige looked her new friend up and down appreciatively—she couldn't help it. He didn't seem to mind. "Yeah, the Internet and I are not friends today," she said, shaking her head sadly. "It's bad news."

"Are you writing a paper?" he asked.

Paige started to shake her head, then realized it was a better cover than the truth. She didn't really want to be talking about the fact that she was digging up dirt on a co-worker. *Or, not digging up dirt, to be more precise,* she amended mentally. "Yeah, well, it's a class in new media, and my paper is on the global community, you know," she ad-libbed. "How we're all connected online. I mean, you can Google just about anyone and you're destined to get a hit or two, right?"

"Yeah, check it out," he said eagerly, leaning over and sending his fingers flying over her keyboard. He typed in "Drew Byars" and hit Enter. Instantly he and Paige were led to an extensive Web site for a surf school, complete with hightech graphics and streaming video. "That's me," he said, tapping the screen where a surfer was riding the inside of a massive wave.

"Drew Byars, I assume?" Piper guessed.

He nodded. "Yup. I'm an amateur surfer and I run a school and a surf shop. You should come by."

"Oh, gee, I, uh . . . don't surf. At all," Paige said quickly.

"You could learn. That's the point," Drew said. He pointed at his chest. "From the almost-master." He made puppy-dog eyes at her. "Come on. What are you doing tomorrow afternoon? You could come down to the shop and I'll hook you up with some rental gear, show you the basics. . . ." He looked at her questioningly. She realized she still hadn't given him her name.

"I'm Paige. Paige Matthews," she finished, extending her hand for a shake that lingered for a moment longer than necessary. "And I really can't. I'd love to, but . . . I'm busy tomorrow.

Um, really busy." Though, if she couldn't get a lead on Katie, what was she really busy doing?

Paige glanced at Drew again. He was *really* cute. And there was something about the surfer thing he had going that appealed to her. Just before she moved into the Manor she had come very close to going traveling with her then-boyfriend, Glen. At the last minute she decided to embrace her destiny as a Charmed One. And sometimes it felt like the sacrifices never ended.

Like now, for instance. There was a good chance that she could spend the next forty-eight hours glued to her computer monitor without finding out anything new about Katie or the Bayside Center. But that didn't mean she could just give up at the first sign of a hottie alert. She sighed again, this time more dramatically. "I can't," she said again, realizing as the words came that, really, she didn't mind that much. It was all part of a day's work as a witch. Which, for the most part, was pretty cool. "But thanks."

"Fine," Drew said, pretending to pout. He reached into the back pocket of his jeans and dug out a business card. It was fluorescent orange and shaped like a surfboard, and it had all of his shop's information printed on its face. "But take this in case you change your mind," he insisted. "Our hours are listed on the card."

Paige nodded and accepted the card from him. "I'll definitely try to stop by soon," she said. "But probably not this weekend."

Drew gathered up his books and a newspaper, which he tucked under one arm, and picked up his cup of coffee with the other. He managed a weak but earnest chin wave at her even though his hands were full. "Cool. Good to meet you, Paige." He turned and left Java Joe's.

Once he had left, Paige allowed herself a moment of silent sulking. Then she turned back to the matter at hand. This time she tried new combinations: "Katie Whitesmith." Nothing. "Whitesmith, Katie." Zip. "K. Whitesmith, RN." Nada.

Paige took a sip of her coffee and contemplated topping her cup off again. It was definitely going to be a long afternoon.

Chapter Six

On Monday morning Paige awoke feeling as though she hadn't slept at all. She knew it was just knots in her stomach about getting to the bottom of what was going on at the day care center, but that didn't make it any easier to drag herself out of bed. She showered and dressed quickly and slipped out of the house before anyone else was even out of bed, not wanting to impose her bad mood on her family.

As she drove off in the direction of the center, she ran through the facts of the situation one more time. *Fact: Piper thinks that Wyatt's been weird ever since she took him home from Bayside. Fact: Two other mothers had the same comment about their children's behaviors. Fact: Katie, who seemed like the perfect child-care professional, up and walked off suddenly, without giving any notice at all.*

She hadn't been able to turn up any information on Katie—weird enough in and of itself—

and her searches on the Bayside Center had really only yielded information about the year it was founded, the board of directors, the trustees, and the center's annual fundraising drive. Not exactly hair-raising stuff, but still. Did it mean something that all of the children who were pulled from the center were babies? Though Katie hadn't ever been an official nursery worker, she had spent most of her down time at the center with the infants.

Paige paused at a red light and tapped her fingernails against the steering wheel in frustration. There was definitely something else going on here. Some piece of the puzzle was missing. But what?

She pulled into the center's back lot and parked her car. She had dressed to be ready for anything: denim capris, a bright, stretchy T-shirt, and comfortable platform slides. She could face kids in heels if she had to, and the same went for evil. But if both were working in tandem? Sensible footwear was required. Paige squared her shoulders and marched toward the back door of the center. Ready for anything was all well and good, but unfortunately she had absolutely no idea what "anything" could entail.

Paige pushed open the door, stepped inside, and gasped. Apparently, "anything" meant a complete and total lack of babies. *No, wait, check that*, she thought quickly. *There's one. No, two.* Through the windowed partitions she could see the usual number of toddlers and young children roaming about their rooms, playing and coloring, but the infant room—except for one slumbering baby—was empty.

Dori stood just outside the nursery, cradling one baby over her shoulder and patting its back. She was cooing and making gentle noises that seemed as much intended for her as for her charge. Paige knew her boss must be freaking. Losing most of their infants—there was no *way* that that wasn't a sign of something big and bad at work.

"Dori, *what* is going on?" Paige demanded, quickly dashing over to where she stood. "Why are there only two babies here?"

Dori looked at Paige sadly. "You were right, Paige. There's been something happening to the babies here. Something about the center that doesn't agree with them. I got in at eight and there were already ten messages on our machine saying that infants weren't coming back again. The same complaints over and over again: The children weren't behaving like themselves, they were cranky, they were fussy. . . . Paige," Dori asked, glancing up again miserably, "is it something we're doing? Are we somehow *ruining* these children's temperaments?"

Paige shook her head emphatically. "No, Dori, *no*. I mean, unfortunately, I have no idea what's going on, but I can promise you that it isn't you. The other groups are being affected too, obviously. And you're amazing with the babies—with all of the kids," she assured her. "We'll figure it out," she said determinedly. *God only knows how,* she thought, deflated.

"Look, I'll start our morning meeting," Paige continued, hoping to jostle Dori out of her mood. "You just . . . stay with the babies. Baby," she quickly corrected herself.

Dori pointed at the infant snoring away in the infant room. "There are two," she said defiantly. "Babies." She shrugged underneath the weight of the baby in her arm. "The last two." She sounded completely defeated and baffled.

Paige patted Dori encouragingly on the back and turned to face the room. Although all of the other children were in attendance, the vibe in the room was tense, like everyone "got" the fact that something was off. "Regan, you are hereby dubbed Kid of the Day," Paige said, completely without the usual fanfare, to a small redhead. She led the short, freckled five-year-old girl to the front of the story mat and walked her through the agenda, praying inwardly that none of the kids would ask about the sudden lack of infants. She wasn't really paying attention, though. She was too busy wracking her brain, trying to figure out a way to steal away at lunch to update her sisters on the situation at the center. She couldn't very well call for Leo or orb herself in front of all the children, and this wasn't a conversation that she really wanted to have over a cell phone.

After Regan finished the agenda, Paige set up the children at their tables with crayons and paper, and started to head off for a quick sip of coffee. As she walked back toward the office she felt a tug at her sleeve, and looked down to see Natalie staring up at her, eyes round as saucers. "What's wrong, honey?" Paige asked gently.

Natalie blinked, looking as if she was going to cry. "Paige, where did all the babies go?" she asked, sounding extremely nervous. "Did something happen to them?"

"What? Oh, of course not, sweetie," Paige said firmly. "Nothing happened to them. Their mommies and daddies just wanted to spend some time with them at home. That's all." She chose her words carefully, wanting to be sure that Natalie understood that no one in the day care center was in any danger—*At least, not that I'm aware of*, she thought fervently,—but also not wanting to suggest in any way that those children who were not pulled from day care were loved by their parents any less. "They'll be back." She crossed her fingers behind her, feeling bad for misleading the young girl. But it was all for the greater good, wasn't it?

"Well . . . ," Natalie said, looking uncomfortable, "I was wondering if the reason that the babies are gone is because . . . well . . ." She looked away.

"What, Natalie? You can tell me. You can tell me anything," Paige assured her.

"Well, I thought maybe they weren't here because of how they were the wrong babies."

"No, of course not—" Paige began automatically. Then she stopped. *What?* What had Natalie just said? "Wrong babies?" *What does* that *mean?* She touched the girl's wrist lightly. "The wrong babies? Natalie, what do you mean?"

Natalie shrugged, looking like she didn't want to say more. "I'm not supposed to talk about it," she whispered.

"What can't you talk about?" Paige asked desperately. "Why not?" Then it dawned on her—the picture with the fairies. Playing house. "You're not supposed to talk about things that you think in your imagination, right? Your parents don't like that?" All at once, everything clicked—just as she'd suspected the other day, Natalie's "imagination" wasn't imagination, after all. She was an Innocent, and a child, which meant that she could see things, like fairies, that adults had long since lost belief in. Adults like Natalie's parents, who didn't want to encourage their daughter's strange ideas.

Natalie nodded. "Mommy and Daddy don't like me to tell other people about the things I see in my imagination. They say I should only tell them."

Paige sighed. "Natalie, normally I would tell you to listen to your parents, but the thing is, you and I both know that some of the things that you can see are not from your imagination— they're real. And sometimes grown-ups can't see them, so they think you're making up stories. But I'm not like other grown-ups. I can see things, too, so I understand what you're talking about and I know that you're telling the truth." Natalie looked immensely relieved. "So why don't you tell me what was wrong with the babies," Paige hedged, smoothing a strand of hair off Natalie's forehead.

"They were switched," Natalie said. "By a little magic person."

"What sort of little magic person?" Paige asked, worried.

"It was Katie, but it wasn't," Natalie said. "She was different."

Paige did not like the sound of that. "Natalie, can you tell me everything that you saw?"

Paige placed the other children—who seemed to be losing interest in coloring—at various stations throughout the room, and once they had all busied themselves with various activities, she led Natalie to one of the small worktables so they could continue their chat. "Start from the beginning," Paige suggested. "And don't be afraid to tell me everything."

"I saw it last week," Natalie said. "Before the . . . before the first babies were gone."

Paige thought back quickly. "Tuesday?" she wondered, remembering that had been Wyatt's last day at the center.

Natalie looked uncertain. "I don't know. It was the end of the day, and you were cleaning up, and Dori was helping Michael change his shirt because of how he spilled the paint."

Paige had to stifle a giggle, remembering that incident. "Definitely Tuesday," she repeated. "How could I forget something like that?"

Natalie took a deep breath and continued. "And Katie went into the infant room, and when no one was looking, she . . . she went fuzzy. She didn't see me peeking at her. And then she turned into something else. I don't know what."

"A fairy?" Paige asked, since Natalie was clearly familiar with fairies.

Natalie laughed. "No! Fairies don't work at day care!" That much was true, Paige had to hand it to her. "I don't know what," Natalie went on. "Something with pointy ears. And short. But mostly the ears were different, and she was wearing different clothing, like pajamas, and she *looked* different. And then she made a little song to herself—but I couldn't hear it—and there was a little light. And all of the babies went fuzzy too. And then there were new babies."

"You could just tell they were new?" Paige asked.

Natalie nodded somewhat proudly. "Because of how they went fuzzy. And the new ones were different."

"But it could have been something that happened to the babies when they 'went fuzzy,'" Paige pointed out. "Not that they were different."

"But then I sneaked over closer to see what was going on, and I could hear Katie talking to the babies," Natalie went on. "And she was calling them different names. I didn't hear everything, but the baby that used to be Simon? She was calling him 'Caleb.'"

Goose bumps broke out over Paige's skin. This could be serious. She was so grateful to finally have some sort of lead that she didn't even stop to be concerned that her information came from a preschooler. She glanced at her watch. It was barely 11:00 AM. But she *had* to get out of there so she could talk to Leo and her sisters. She had to tell them what Natalie had said!

Then it hit her: She'd been so worried about the babies, she hadn't thought about the one baby that meant the most to her and her sisters—Wyatt! Was he "wrong" too?

She knew Dori would freak at being left alone at the center. But it just didn't matter. Wyatt was her top priority.

She turned to Natalie. "I want you to know that you did the right thing, telling me the truth," she explained to the girl. "You can always tell me anything. Even if it's something you imagined." She hugged Natalie, then raced to the nursery room to talk to Dori.

"Look, I'm really sorry, and I know it's bad timing, but I *really* have to go," she said. "My sister is, um . . . home with Wyatt, and she's not feeling well. She needs help, and I really can't leave her alone."

Dori looked appalled. "Paige, you can't just *leave* in the middle of the day!" she said. "Especially not when we're short staffed."

"I know, and I'm *really* sorry," Paige repeated. "This is lousy timing. But I can't help it." Before Dori could protest further, Paige grabbed her keys and her bag and darted off to her car.

"Change, change, change," Paige muttered to the traffic light, frustrated. She was only blocks from the Manor, but it felt like she'd been in the car for hours. She was desperate to get home and see Wyatt—or, whatever had replaced him. She didn't know, of course, whether the new creature was dangerous or otherwise evil. And Piper was home alone with Wyatt, with no idea what was going on!

She grabbed at her cell phone and quickly punched in Phoebe's number at work.

"Phoebe Halliwell," her sister barked into the phone after just one ring. Phoebe sounded stressed. Paige hated to bother her—she knew how precious their "normal lives" were to each of them—but certain things were too important to ignore, and when it came down to it, Charmed duties always came first.

"Phoebes, it's me. I need you to meet me back at the Manor ASAP," Paige said breathlessly. The light changed and she accelerated.

Phoebe groaned loudly into the phone. "Paige, I can't. I have a staff meeting in ten minutes. Elise will kill me if I miss it. Plus, my column is still overdue. I'm gonna be here all night."

"Hmm, well, in that case, I have some good news, and I have some bad news. The good news is you probably *won't* be there all night," Paige said. "If my lead pans out, you'll definitely be doing the Charmed and Dangerous thing at home."

"So what's the bad news?" Phoebe half shouted.

"Well, the Charmed and Dangerous thing," Paige said.

"What? What's that supposed to mean?" Phoebe demanded. Paige could hear a rustle of papers that definitely meant Phoebe was frantically flipping through her afternoon schedule.

"Look, I really don't want to get into it over the phone, but I think Piper's hunch about Wyatt may be true. I think he's really not . . . himself. In the supernatural sense. In which case there's a really good chance that we're going to need the Power of Three. Just trust me. And *come home.*"

There was a bang that sounded like the close of a desk drawer. "Okay, now you're scaring me," Phoebe said. "I'm on my way. But if I get fired, you're going to have to hook me up with that temp agency."

"Not a problem," Paige said. "Come to think of it, there's an opening at the Bayside Child Care Center." She sighed. "Possibly two."

"Piper!" Paige called, rushing through the front door of the Manor. She'd spent her entire car ride home speculating as to what sort of monster the Wyatt-baby actually was, and she was terrified she'd come home to total destruction. She was unprepared to find Piper at home, sitting at the kitchen table, forlornly stirring a mug of tea. "Piper! What's wrong?"

"I give up," Piper said, dejected. "Nothing I do for Wyatt makes him happy. We've had another awful morning. I'm apparently unable to figure out my own son's needs, and I'm exhausted from trying. It was a toss-up who'd pass out first."

"Wait," Paige said, "don't panic. It's not you. I think you're right. I think there's something really wrong with Wyatt. I mean, I think that might not even *be* Wyatt up there."

"What? What are you talking about?" Piper shrieked, immediately getting to her feet. "LEO!" she called urgently into the air.

It only took a moment for Leo to materialize. "What is it, Piper?" he asked, concerned. At the same time, Phoebe walked in, looking ready for business, and sat down at the table.

"Paige says there's something wrong with Wyatt," Piper said, hand on one hip. "I think there's finally real cause for concern."

"Well, given that you dragged me from my desk—and my *serious* writer's block—I'm sort of glad to hear it. . . . You know . . . in a weird way," Phoebe confessed. "He wasn't any better today?" she asked, shooting her sister an anxious look. Piper's glare was all the answer she needed.

Paige crossed her arms over her chest and explained to her sisters and Leo what she'd learned, up to and including her chat with Natalie.

"So, a toddler tells you that the babies are 'wrong,' that they were switched, and what's-her-name 'changed' the other day," Phoebe recapped.

Paige nodded. "I'm thinking it must have been Tuesday, and while she was changed, she switched all the babies. I don't know what that means. But there's a good chance that either the babies are not the babies that we think they are, or that if they are, they've been worked over with some sort of magic mojo." Paige took a deep breath and leveled Piper with a meaningful gaze. "And that includes Wyatt."

Leo frowned. "If it were something large scale, the Elders would have told me, wouldn't they?" he thought aloud.

"Wait, wait a minute . . . ," Phoebe said, waving a finger in the air. "We're still talking about a four-year-old with a vivid imagination being our sole source of info."

"And a very cranky baby who's proving this theory true," Piper said with an exhausted sigh.

"Okay, let's go on the assumption that you're right—you and your little informant," Phoebe said, relenting. "Now that I think of it, I do remember there being something in the Book of Shadows about someone . . . or some group . . . that swaps babies. They take the babies of others and leave their own behind. The ones they leave behind are usually camouflaged with a glamour or something. And I think they're called 'changelings.'" She looked at Paige. "Did Natalie say anything about what Katie, or whoever it was, looked like?"

Paige shrugged. "Small. Pointy ears." She looked at her sisters meaningfully. "Like an elf, I think."

"No way," Piper said. "It doesn't make sense. First of all, wouldn't Wyatt's force field have gone up? Nothing can harm that kid. And meanwhile—aren't elves creatures of good?"

Leo looked very excited. "Yes, but they *are* known for mischief. And it may be that the changeling swap is more about wreaking havoc than spreading evil."

"Well, they're wreaking with the wrong witches," Piper snapped. "And that still doesn't explain how she got around Wyatt's force field," she insisted.

Leo shook his head. "No, Wyatt's defenses

would have been down if the elf was a shape-shifter and someone he trusted."

"Like Katie," Paige said, slapping her palm against her forehead. "He would have trusted Katie. I mean, we worked side by side at the center. *I* trusted Katie! Ugh, this is all my fault!"

"Hey, hey, hey," Piper exclaimed, walking over to put her arm around Paige. "Not a chance. If it's anyone's fault, it's mine, for being so quick to race back to work that I passed Wyatt off at the first chance I got."

"Wait a minute, now, you were just doing what lots of working mothers do," Phoebe said. "No reason to beat yourself up."

"Ladies, I think we're missing the point here," Leo said, trying to steer everyone back to the matter at hand.

"You're right. Book of Shadows?" Phoebe asked, pointing her finger at the ceiling and leading the way up the stairs to the attic.

"Keep it quiet though," Piper said, shushing them as they made their way up the staircase. "Wyatt—or whatever it is that's posing as my son—is sleeping."

Upstairs, Phoebe stood over the book and began flipping pages. "I think it was in the 'elves' section," she said. She stopped on a page and stabbed her finger down onto the paper. "'Changelings,'" she read. She scanned the entry. "Okay, yeah. 'Mischievous elves have been known to exchange their own babies for those of other species for the sole purpose of creating harmless havoc.' Harmless!" she exclaimed.

"Does it say anything about how to get our babies back?" Piper prodded her.

Phoebe looked back at the entry. "Well, first we have to make sure it *is* a changeling. We can say a spell that will reveal the baby's true face."

"Let's do it," Paige said, clapping her hands together.

Piper darted downstairs to rouse Wyatt from his nap. Moments later she re-emerged in the attic carrying a bleary-eyed baby that was an exact replica of her natural-born son. "I just can't believe that this could be an elf, rather than my child," Piper mused. "And yet . . . I guess I can believe it. I sort of *want* to believe it. It would explain so much." She took a deep breath. "Say the spell, Phoebe."

Phoebe stepped forward and held her palms flat over Wyatt's head.

> *"Forces of darkness,*
> *Forces of light,*
> *Pull back the curtain*
> *To reveal what is right."*

A flash of light burst through the room, and Piper was enveloped in a thick cloud of smoke.

When the smoke cleared, Piper stood, as before, holding an infant—an infant with short, stocky limbs, pointed ears, twinkling pink eyes, and sharp little teeth peeking over his bottom lip. The infant opened his mouth and giggled.

Chapter Seven

Even though she expected something to happen after the spell was performed, Piper was so startled she almost dropped the baby. Fortunately Paige was thinking on her feet. "Baby," she called, orbing the elf into her own arms. The baby squealed with elfish delight as Paige's arms wrapped around him. She shuddered. "Oooh, *so* creepy. Okay, to start with, great, here's an elf . . . but where's Wyatt? And, I mean, I don't have anything against elves—or, at least, I didn't until this little incident—but can we put him down somewhere? I'm icked out."

"Paige, we've got bigger problems than an icky elf baby," Piper said, sounding slightly hysterical. Leo came around next to his wife and wrapped his arms around her waist.

"Don't panic, Piper," he said calmly. "It won't help us to get Wyatt back."

"We don't even know where he is," she muttered, sounding hopeless.

"Well, we have a pretty good lead," Leo replied logically. "Not to mention, our boy is pretty powerful. You and I both know that he can take care of himself until we find him."

"True," Piper said, feeling slightly more subdued. "But let's get to him sooner rather than later, okay?"

Leo kissed her forehead. "Of course," he agreed.

"I'll scry for the elves," Paige offered.

"Most elves cloak their villages to protect them," Leo pointed out. "You can scry for the general vicinity, and then we'll have to go there and say a spell if we want the entrance to the village to be revealed."

"Why all the secrecy? So they can run around stealing babies unimpeded?" Phoebe asked wryly.

"Actually, elves really are basically good creatures," Leo explained. The sisters looked at him with skepticism. "It's true. Though I don't blame you if you aren't feeling very sympathetic. They cloak their village with a glamour to protect themselves from malevolent beings. They just want to live their lives alone and unbothered."

"You're starting to sound like you work for People for the Ethical Treatment of Elves," Piper grumbled.

"I'm scrying," Paige said hastily as she handed the baby off to a squeamish Piper. "I want my nephew back, and I want some answers." She took out their map of the Bay Area and walked over to the window seat, unfolded the paper, reached and took the scrying crystal off its hook, and dangled it over the map until it was forcefully drawn to a particular location. "And, we have a winner!" she exclaimed triumphantly. "Leo was right. It's the woods, behind Golden Gate Park. Do we have a spell?"

"The one Phoebe used to reveal the changeling should do the trick. It's about lifting the veil to reveal reality," Leo suggested. "That should work fine for you."

"What do you mean, 'for you'?" Piper asked. "I'm going to rescue our son. Where were you planning to be?"

Leo pointed toward the ceiling. "Up there. Now that we've got concrete evidence, I'm going to see if the Elders can fill me in on any of this. It couldn't hurt. You don't *really* need me there, right? Elves aren't actually evil, and you're going in with the Power of Three. Call if you need me."

Phoebe stood up straight, assuming her boss position. "Okay, you," she said, pointing to Leo. "Get up there and get the skinny. Piper's got the baby; Paige, grab that spell and orb us outta here. We've got to go kick a little elf butt." Leo nodded and orbed off.

"They *do* have little ones, I'm guessing," Paige joked as she scribbled quickly from the Book of Shadows. "That's one thing working in our favor." Her sisters turned to glare at her in tandem, and she opened her eyes wide in protest. "What? Just trying to lighten the tension, okay? Jeez."

"Whatever," Piper said, straining under the weight of her pointy-eared charge. "This kid is *not* light. Can we step on it?"

Paige laughed nervously, and they all orbed away.

The scrying map had led the girls to the deepest thicket in the woods, a nook just behind Golden Gate Park where the canopy of trees looked dense enough to walk upon. The deep cover of the woods gave them the creeps, even in broad daylight. Each of them had had at least one harrowing experience in the woods at one point or another and wasn't eager to be reminded of it.

"Are you sure this is the spot?" Piper asked, sounding uncertain. It was so quiet and placid there in the daytime. The elf baby was strapped securely into a Snugli, facing out from Piper's chest, bobbing up and down peacefully. Thankfully no one had seen them park and walk by. They'd had to explain away a lot in the time since their powers had been activated, but a baby with Spock ears and canine incisors was going to be hard to hide.

Phoebe didn't look especially sure this was the spot. "Um, not so much," she confessed. "But it's where the crystal led us, so, yeah. Here we are." She reached into her pocket and unfolded a square of paper—a crumpled receipt Paige had found on the attic floor. She smoothed it out and cleared her throat. "Here goes nothing," she said.

> *"Forces of darkness,*
> *Forces of light,*
> *Pull back the curtain*
> *To reveal what is right."*

Boom! Another flash of light exploded, and a cloud of smoke billowed around the girls. Phoebe began coughing. "Did we do it?" she asked.

"Oh, my," Piper responded.

Phoebe looked up to see what her sister was reacting to and gasped. Before them lay an entire elf village; a small series of interconnected cottages with thatched roofs and arched wooden doorways that reminded Phoebe of something out of *Lord of the Rings*. That, or *The Smurfs*. "It's teeny tiny!" she exclaimed, sounding delighted.

"Yeah, adorable," Piper quipped. "Let's find my kid."

"Uh, I don't think we're going to have to look that far," Paige said, sounding nervous. She pointed straight ahead. "Someone found us."

Indeed, a small team of pointy-eared creatures were rushing toward them wildly. "Who goes there?" called one, a man with thick, curly black hair and a beard to match.

"We're witches," Paige said. "You may have heard of us. The Charmed Ones. We have one of your babies."

The elf stopped running and hunched over, leaning his palms on his knees and breathing heavily. "Must get back into shape," he muttered. Once his breathing pattern had returned to normal, he looked up at the sisters again. "How did you find us? You must be creatures of magic," he accused. His small cadre of elf friends caught up to him and gathered around the girls in a completely nonthreatening semicircle.

"You bet your little elf—," Piper began, stepping forward.

Paige held out an arm. "Piper . . ." She turned to the elf. "Pay attention this time. We're witches. Take us to your leader, or find me someone who can."

The bearded elf squinted at her. "Why would we do that?" His gaze traveled to the baby dangling from Piper's torso, noticing it for the first time "Why do you have our baby?" Realization dawned across his face slowly.

Phoebe raised an eyebrow at the elf. "I think the real question is, why do *you* have *our* baby?"

"And all of the babies I worked with at the Bayside Child Care Center?" Paige added.

The elf ignored Paige's accusations and ran to Piper to have a closer look at the little boy-elf in her arms. "Samuel!" he said happily. "You're all right!"

"Yeah, buddy, and you'd better hope for your sake that Wyatt is too," Piper growled. "And that there's a really good explanation for all of this."

The elf looked uneasy. "Did you say 'Charmed Ones'?" he asked.

Piper nodded. "That's what the woman said."

He turned back toward the village, gesturing for them to follow him. "This way."

Rowan, the elf king, was not especially imposing. It didn't help that he was about three feet tall. He sat on a small, plush throne in a special cottage decorated with gilded trim and lush red carpeting. The sisters nearly sank into the floor as they made their way to see him.

"I understand you are not happy with us," Rowan said, waving a tiny brass-colored scepter in their direction.

"Understatement of the year, bub," Piper said, gesturing at the baby she carried. "I'll swap you one Samuel for my son, Wyatt. And for your sake, you'd better hope that there's not a single hair on his head out of place."

Phoebe nodded conspiratorially. "And believe me, we'll know if there is."

"It's not just Wyatt," Paige reminded everyone. "Almost all of the babies at the center disappeared. They must be here somewhere."

Rowan nodded grimly. "I know it wasn't right, but you don't understand the situation. . . . You don't know what this would have meant. . . ." He sighed, and stepped grandly down from his throne. "They're here. They're fine. They're with Caitlyn in the nursery. I'll take you myself."

He made his way through a series of winding passages, the girls following with slight trepidation. Rowan himself didn't seem dangerous, and besides, they'd dealt with elves before. Ironically, when Piper needed extra help with Wyatt, she had called the best nanny she knew—an elf.

"Here we are," Rowan said, pausing before a thick wooden door. "This is the nursery." He puffed out his chest and pushed himself against the door with all of his might. It swung open with a heavy creaking sound. "Caitlyn, please bring me the baby called Wyatt," he called out.

The sisters crouched down, entered the nursery, and gasped.

"Wyatt!" Paige called, inadvertently orbing him into her arms. She held him out for Piper, who pelted his face with kisses.

"Oh, my goodness," said Caitlyn, the elf nanny on duty. She rushed forward and removed Samuel from Piper's Snugli. "How did you find us?"

Piper glared at her. "I hate to break it to you, sister, but you messed with the wrong humans."

She hugged Wyatt close to her chest. "This is my son, and"—Piper nodded to her sisters—"we're the Charmed Ones."

Caitlyn gasped.

"The question is, why did you take any of them?" Phoebe added. "Just for kicks? 'Cause there are a lot of unhappy humans out there beyond your village. And you know we can't let you get away with this."

"Katie?" Paige asked, incredulous. She moved closer to the elf, scrutinizing her face carefully. "You're Katie, aren't you? You're the one who switched the babies at the center!"

The elf nanny's face crumpled, and she began to cry. "It's true. I did switch them. But it wasn't just for fun! I had to! Tell them, Rowan," she said pleadingly.

Rowan shrugged and pulled thoughtfully at his silver-tipped beard. "It is true. We were in a difficult position," he agreed.

"I thought elves were into mischief," Phoebe asked. "You're saying it was more than that?"

Rowan nodded, gesturing to all the babies in the nursery. They were gurgling happily in their bassinets, looking peaceful and well cared for. "Does it look like we hurt them? Caitlyn is a top child-care professional." Caitlyn swelled with pride despite her tears.

"I'm sorry, but that doesn't really matter," Piper said. "We've got to return these kids to their parents."

"*All* of them," Paige said, stunned at how many rows of human babies lay before her. She did a quick tally and guesstimated that there were about a hundred infants in the nursery. At least five times the number of babies she'd worked with. "These babies weren't all from the Bayside Center, were they?" she accused.

Caitlyn dropped her head, ashamed. "No. I had to go to a few different places. I needed an army."

"An army of *babies*?" Piper asked with disbelief. "What would elves do with an army of babies?"

"We had no choice," Rowan repeated. "A demon bounty hunter descended upon our village. She wanted our offspring. One of the lords of the Underworld is amassing an army from the ground up, and he wanted our children."

"So you offered him human babies instead," Phoebe guessed. "Oooh, I don't like this."

"And most humans don't have magical powers, either," Paige said. "Was he planning on giving them powers? Without powers, an underworldly army isn't really worth jack."

"I think he was going to give them powers," Caitlyn confirmed. "Though we don't know anything more. The bounty hunter really didn't have any information for us."

"So you just bartered off human babies?" Piper asked, shocked. "And now you're telling us you had no choice? Like we're supposed to be supportive, or feel sorry for you, or something?"

"What were we to do?" Rowan asked.

"You could have come to us. Lots of Innocents do, and we help them," Phoebe reminded him gently. "We could have faced the bounty hunter or the demon for you, and the babies would have been safe. Stealing human children was *not* the answer."

"And you're going to have to switch them back," Piper demanded.

Caitlyn swallowed hard. "Then what will we do when the bounty hunter comes back?"

"Not my problem anymore," Piper said. "Apparently, you can work these things out on your own."

"She'll kill us all!" Caitlyn said, sounding frantic.

"You stole human babies to give to a demon army general," Piper reminded her. "Given that *someone* was bound to notice, you should've had a plan B. You can work on that once you send the other babies back."

"I can't do that from here," Caitlyn said petulantly.

"Now, I know that's not true," Paige interjected. "Natalie said you 'went blurry' at the center, and then made all the babies go blurry, and you sang a little song, and that's how they changed. I'm thinking you've got some sort of fairy dust—"

"*Elf* dust—" Rowan sniffed.

"—that you use to swap the babies magically," Paige went on, ignoring the king's interruption.

Caitlyn looked huffy. "*That's* how you found me out? A little girl?"

"Don't worry, we would have figured it out on our own eventually," Phoebe said. "Piper knows her own son." *Even if we were too stubborn to trust her instincts right away,* she thought with remorse. She shot her sister a forgive-me-for-blowing-off-your-concerns look, but Piper smiled in a way that said it wasn't even necessary.

Caitlyn sighed, resigned to her fate. "Stand back," she told the sisters, who each took a giant step back toward the door. She reached into her pocket and plucked out a stash of elf dust, leaned forward, and blew lightly on her hand. The dust flew out in all directions and, much as Natalie had reported, the scene seemed to shimmer and melt momentarily. Once the glitter dust had dissipated, the sisters could see that the elves had been returned to their bassinets.

"Weren't they camouflaged?" Phoebe asked. "To look like humans?"

"Yes, but the magics reverse when the babies are back in our kingdom," Rowan explained.

Caitlyn's shoulders slumped. "We've done your bidding; if you're not interested in helping us, you may go now. The bounty hunter should be here in a few hours, and we must prepare.

She will not be happy with us—but I will not let her take our babies."

"Then you understand how we feel," Phoebe said gently. "We can't help you. You threatened human babies," she finished. "We'll go now."

"I can show you to the front gates of the village," Rowan said. "Once you've stepped beyond them, you'll be outside of our magical cloak. You won't be able to see the village again without your spell."

"Okey-doke," Piper said, eager to get Wyatt home to see his daddy.

"Good luck with the bounty hunter," Paige said, feeling slightly guilty about leaving the elves to fend for themselves. After all, they seemed so small and innocent. *Of course, if they were innocent, they wouldn't have stolen an entire army of human babies,* she thought, steeling herself.

Rowan led the sisters down a winding, rocky path. As they drew farther from the village the path became more and more overgrown. Finally they found the gates of the village. Rowan pushed the doors open for them.

"I apologize again for this terrible incident," he said. "I hope you understand that our hands were tied."

"And I hope *you* understand why we couldn't let you go through with it," Piper said. Wyatt grinned at Rowan from the safety of his Snugli.

Rowan nodded grimly. "Be safe," he said. He

stepped aside to let the sisters pass through.

Once they'd passed beyond the gate, they turned back to see the village once more. As Rowan had explained, it was hidden again.

"Come on, guys," Piper said, dusting her hands off on the sides of her jeans. "Let's get Wyatt home."

"Guess who's home!" Piper shouted, walking through the front door of the Manor. Her voice echoed off the walls of the hallway. "Leo?" He was nowhere to be found. Piper stepped into the living room and tried once again for good measure. "Leo!"

Phoebe and Paige followed close on her heels. "Maybe he's still Up There," Phoebe suggested.

"How anticlimactic," Piper grumbled, collapsing into a living-room chair.

Just as she began to unstrap Wyatt from his Snugli, the room was bathed in soft white light. Leo materialized, looking confused and worried. "Piper?" he asked. Then he saw Wyatt and a huge grin erupted across his face. "There's my guy!" he exclaimed, scooping his son up into a bear hug. "Did you miss us?" he asked. He whirled back to face Piper. "He's all right, isn't he?"

Piper nodded wearily. "Yup. They were treating him like a king, even though they had no idea who he was. Wyatt was only one of about a hundred babies the elves had switched for—get this—"

"An army for the Underworld, right?" Leo

finished for her. "The Elders just got a line on this one. They were furious. In a way, it's a good thing the elves took Wyatt, or we might not have gotten to the bottom of their scheme."

"Yeah, fab," Piper said sarcastically.

"And you were able to get them to switch the babies back?" Leo asked.

Paige nodded. "They were not pleased about it. They're very concerned about what's going to happen when the bounty hunter comes."

Leo nodded. "And with good reason. They really only practice low-level magic. They can't protect themselves against the bounty hunter."

Phoebe bit her lip nervously. "So, what are you saying? That we should have offered to stay and help?"

Leo looked at them incredulously. "Of course. You're the Charmed Ones—the protectors of Innocents. The elves are Innocents."

"It's not that simple, Leo," Piper protested. "They stole our son and a lot of other humans. They were going to give our babies to a demonic bounty hunter. That sort of takes away from the whole 'Innocent' thing, don't you think?"

"They made a mistake, Piper, there's no denying that. And I don't blame you for being furious. What you do is your call. I'm just telling you where the Elders stand."

"And where do *you* stand?" Piper pressed.

Paige cleared her throat. "Look, I, uh, didn't want to say anything back there—because

you're right, what the elves did was terrible—
but yeah, I feel sorry for them. And I'm worried
for them. And I *really* didn't like just walking
away and leaving them to fend for themselves."

Piper whirled to face her sister. "So you think
we should go back?"

Phoebe raised her hand meekly. "I sort of do
too," she said. "Am I a traitor auntie?"

Piper scowled at her sisters, and then slowly
raised her own hand into the air. "Me three," she
confessed. "I've been feeling rotten ever since
we left. I just didn't want to say anything."

"When did Caitlyn say the bounty hunter
was coming?" Paige asked.

"In a few hours," Phoebe said. "Which doesn't
give us much time to get ready."

"Bounty hunters can be scary, but they're
usually just your basic mercenary demons," Leo
said. "A simple Power of Three spell should do
the trick."

"I can whip up a quick vanquishing potion,
just in case," Paige offered.

"Can you hurry?" Piper asked.

Paige nodded grimly. "Of course."

The second time around, the sisters were well
familiar with the layout of the elf village. Which
was good, because they didn't have a moment to
spare. Leo had stayed behind with Wyatt.
Someone had to, and Leo figured it was a good
way to catch up on quality time with his son.

This way, the Power of Three stayed intact, and he could always orb to them, if need be.

Stepping through the thick grass carpeting of the village, Phoebe put her hand up to her forehead to shield her eyes from the sun. "Where do you think they would be?" she asked. She quickly checked her watch. "The bounty hunter must be here. Or if not, she's gonna be here really soon."

Paige shrugged helplessly. "The king's quarters?" she suggested.

Piper glanced across the landscape. "I don't know, guys. This isn't looking good. I mean, you could hear a pin drop around here. Where's our Welcome Wagon?"

The girls exchanged a look. "Let's hit the nursery," Phoebe decided. "That's where the bounty hunter would go, right?"

Paige and Piper nodded. It made as much sense as any other plan. In the interest of time, Paige wrapped her arms around her sisters and orbed them off.

Walking into the nursery was like stepping onto the set of a B-level horror movie. Rowan and a small army of officials stood in a protective semicircle around the baby bassinets. Caitlyn was frozen against the far wall, encased in an energy shell that glowed a fizzy eggplant shade. The sisters quickly assessed the situation, following the stream of energy that kept Caitlyn pinned in the corner. It emanated from the flat, outstretched palm of what could only be the demonic bounty hunter.

The bounty hunter was far more frightening than the elf army could ever hope to be. She was impossibly tall and razor thin, her comic-book-villainess figure enhanced by a sleek black jumpsuit. Her hair was wound tightly in a long and low ponytail, but the sisters could make out strands of silver intertwined throughout the inky mass. Her eyes glittered a dull gray shade, and her cheekbones were sharp as knives.

Phoebe took a deep breath and launched herself airborne, levitating across the room to land a solid kick straight at the bounty hunter's waist, sending her reeling backward and breaking the flow of energy that was imprisoning Caitlyn. The bounty hunter stumbled back, then looked up angrily. She wound her arm backward and let go with a crackling energy ball. Piper stepped forward and flicked her hands at it, causing it to explode in thin air.

"Wh-who are you?" the bounty hunter asked in disbelief.

"The Charmed Ones," Piper said simply. "And you would be? . . ."

The bounty hunter reached back again to take another shot with an energy ball. This time Piper reached out and froze the demon. "She's not very friendly," she commented lightly, turning toward Rowan and his army.

Rowan grinned. "You came back! Thank heavens!"

"Yeah, well, the Elders got on our conscience," Piper said. "Let's just say you owe us one." She turned back to the frozen bounty hunter. "Who exactly is this chick?"

"She goes by the name of Mya," Caitlyn said weakly, pulling herself back to her feet. One of the soldiers rushed to help support her. "We don't know where she comes from or who she works for."

"She's just a gun for hire," Rowan explained. "She says she isn't interested in the details of her cases. She just wants the money. The less she knows about the particulars, the better."

"Hmmm. Sorry, but we're gonna need a little more information than that," Piper decided. She reached out and unfroze Mya from the neck up. "Lightning girl—what's your deal?" she asked.

"My 'deal'?" Mya replied witheringly.

"Yeah. As in, who hired you, why, yadda yadda . . . ," Piper explained. "Inquiring minds want to know."

"What business is it of yours?" Mya said coldly.

Phoebe stepped forward, hands on her hips. "It became our business the minute my nephew became involved."

Mya sighed. "Like I told Caitlyn Poppins here, I don't get involved. I don't ask questions.

It's better that way. I just do the job and get gone. What do I know about your nephew?"

"Nothing," Paige agreed. "And we're going to keep it that way. But first we want to know the name of the demon that hired you."

Mya shook her head as best as she could despite the deep freeze. "Not a chance."

"Fine, then," Piper said, sounding tired. "We'll do this the hard way. One . . . ," she counted, "two . . ." She raised a questioning eyebrow in Mya's direction. Mya looked away, her expression like chiseled stone. "Three," Piper finished. With a flick of her wrist she exploded the bounty hunter, leaving the nursery covered in heavy debris.

"She's gone?" Caitlyn coughed. "She's really gone?"

"Well, they don't usually survive *that*," Phoebe explained. "So yeah. You're safe."

"Well, she was working for someone," Rowan pointed out. "Whoever she was working for may send someone else."

Piper nodded thoughtfully. "That's true. But for now, we've bought some time."

"We'll figure it out," Paige promised. "In the meantime can you guys put up a few more magical safeguards around here? We'll go back to the Manor and see what we can find out. We'll be back when we've got some answers."

Rowan nodded. "That shouldn't be too difficult. Although I don't know how long they'll hold."

"A day or two is probably all we need," Paige said. "At most."

"I'll talk to the council sorcerers," Rowan said. "They should be able to come up with something."

The girls turned to go.

"Ladies," Caitlyn called, as they were on their way out. "That was most impressive."

Phoebe shrugged. "It's what we do."

Rowan executed a short bow for their benefit. "I can't thank you enough," he said. His men fell in line and bowed as well.

Piper winked. "Probably not," she said. She smiled to show she was kidding. "But thanks for trying."

Chapter Eight

"Okay, so, I'll be home in a few hours," Piper said, somehow managing to walk into the kitchen, smooth down her hair, and hook an earring into her right earlobe all at the same time. She did a little twirl for Phoebe's benefit. "Presentable?"

"More than presentable—you're a babe. A total hot mama," Phoebe confirmed. Piper was back in career-woman gear: slim-fitting dark jeans and a sheer black top over a spaghetti-strapped camisole. She wore bold silver jewelry and a touch more makeup than usual, and her hair was blown out to a silky sheen.

"Thanks. Every time I'm away from the club for more than a day I worry that I'm losing my grasp of what the cool kids are wearing now," Piper joked. "Have I mentioned it's really hard to balance motherhood with a career?"

"Come to think of it, I believe you have said

something about that once or twice," Phoebe
replied, pretending to look deep in thought.
"Anyway, you earned this—well, I guess it's the
opposite of a break—but you earned it either
way. I mean, you spent the weekend with a
demon baby!"

"Not a demon, an elf," Piper corrected her.
"Not quite the same thing."

"You're right," Phoebe agreed. "But the point
is, I'm glad you're going in to the club today. I
think it will help keep you sane."

"That's assuming I still *have* my sanity," Piper
quipped wryly. "Anyway, I really appreciate
your offering to watch Wyatt. Leo is up with the
Elders trying to get to the bottom of which
demon is after the elf babies, and Paige is working, and, well . . . I just didn't feel comfortable
sending Wyatt back to day care."

"Please. I don't blame you," Phoebe said.
"Even if Wyatt's fine, *I'm* scarred from that experience. Anyway, I'm glad to do it. I love spending time with him, and I can probably do some
research on the demon too. Also, I told Elise I'd
work from home this afternoon."

"How's your column going?" Piper asked.

Phoebe shrugged sheepishly and ran her fingers through her hair. "I'm still having major
writer's block," she confessed. "Normally it just
goes away on its own, but lately I've been getting all of these letters from new moms who are
thrown by the experience, and I have *no* idea

what to tell them. I thought I had all the answers, considering how much time I spend with Wyatt, but I obviously thought wrong." She rested her chin in her hands dejectedly.

"Well, then I guess it's a good thing that you're spending the afternoon with him, right?" Piper said. "Firsthand field research!"

Phoebe perked up slightly. "Definitely."

Piper cocked an eyebrow at her sister. "Or am I just trying to ease my guilt from saddling you with my kid?"

"No, no guilt!" Phoebe insisted, rising from her chair and plucking Wyatt from his swing. "I'm really into staying home with him. We're gonna have a great time—aren't we?" she cooed, smiling at Wyatt, who squealed with delight in response.

"Excellent, that's exactly the response I was looking for," Piper said, scooping up a lipstick and her keys and dropping them into her purse. "All I have to do is check on a few things and meet with a band manager about some scheduling, and then I'll be home. It seriously won't be more than three hours, tops. Call me if something comes up, okay?"

"We will be *fine*," Phoebe said emphatically. "Go." She pointed at the door authoritatively. "Now."

Piper leaned forward and kissed Wyatt noisily. To Phoebe she said, "You're a lifesaver," and rushed out the back door.

Phoebe turned to Wyatt. "Did you hear that, kid? I'm a lifesaver," she said. "Unfortunately I'm also supposed to be a writer. And that part? Yeah, it's not going so well." She carried Wyatt into the living room and deposited him in his playpen, then brought her laptop over to the couch, flipping it open and turning it on. She looked at her nephew, who was peering at her with curiosity. "You can be my muse," she told him. "How does that sound?"

Wyatt giggled in response. Encouraging, sure, but not really the solution to her problem. What to tell these new mothers? Her experience was so limited. Wyatt was only a few months old, after all. She drummed her fingertips against the edges of her computer. Did she know anyone with infants? Did Piper know any new mommies? Surely she did. Maybe the moms had advice. Maybe they were big old fonts of resources. They probably exchanged thoughts and ideas on the way in and out of day care, or Mommy and Me, or doctors' offices. . . . They probably helped each other out. Or so one would think.

Phoebe sat straight up in her seat, a thought coming to her suddenly. She raised her hands, fingers poised over the keyboard.

New moms probably had a lot of opportunities to see one another and to talk about their own experiences. But that didn't necessarily mean that they *took* those opportunities, did it?

Phoebe reached over to the end table and grabbed her glasses. She put them on and opened up a new Word document on her computer.

Then she started to type.

Piper gave the bar one last wipedown with a damp rag and stood back. She had to admit that P3 was looking good—proof positive that with the right staff in place, the club could certainly function without her. She had flipped through the books since she'd gotten in and was thrilled to discover that they'd turned a pretty profit in the few days she'd been home with Wyatt. She sighed. Maybe it *was* time to start thinking more seriously about compromise. After all, the whole one-or-the-other thing hadn't been running so smoothly, had it?

Piper stashed the rag under the bar and glanced at her watch again: 3:45. Her meeting with the band manager had been set for 3:30. She was used to *bands* showing up late—creative types had a problem with deadlines, she'd learned quickly enough—but the managers were usually pathologically punctual. It was something in their managerial blood. Oh, well. She'd be home soon enough.

The front door swung open and someone walked in. Piper looked up to see a man walking toward her with an air of self-confidence and professionalism. He was on the shorter side, but not alarmingly so, and wore clean, dark cords and a button-down shirt tucked in and belted. His thick black hair was stylishly mussed, but not too "done." He was either the band manager, or a petite male model trawling for work. All things considered, Piper had to assume the former.

"Troy?" Piper guessed, stepping out from behind the bar to greet him. "Troy Harper?" She reached out to shake his hand, and he obliged with a firm grip. Suddenly she felt like Businesswoman of the Year again, in control and on top of things, in direct contrast to her bumbling debacle with the delivery man last week. God, it was a great feeling. "Piper Halliwell, owner and manager of this place. Glad to meet you."

"Glad to be here," Troy acknowledged with a short nod. He quickly surveyed the layout of the club. "I like the use of space," he commented. "Did you design it yourself?"

Piper shook her head. "Well, I'm not an architect or an interior designer, but I did have a hand in it, of course." *Understatement of the year*, Piper thought, wondering where her false modesty was coming from. She'd spent countless hours poring over floor plans, fabric swatches, and product samples, until P3 was the exact realization of her dreams. "I wanted to keep the place open enough that dancing and live music wouldn't be an issue," she said simply.

"I'd say you've succeeded," Troy sa. cerely. "I've heard great things about this p. Bands really enjoy performing here."

"And I hope"—Piper wracked her brain for a moment to be sure she got the name right—"that the Pretty Little Devils will too."

"I'm sure," Troy said. "And I've got their schedule programmed into my Palm so we can go over dates and figure out what works best."

Piper smiled. "Let's go back to my office, then, so I can call up the club calendar on the computer." She turned and waved for him to follow her.

Troy held back for a moment. "Piper, is anyone else here?" he asked.

Piper whirled around to face him again. *What an odd question*, she thought fleetingly. She decided he was just trying to get the lay of the land, to figure out who his point people would be, and pushed the flash of unease aside. "Nope, just the two of us. The evening staff comes on in about an hour to start setting up, but I'm going to take off shortly. Got to get home to my son. I'll be long gone by the time the club opens."

A slow smile spread across Troy's face, causing Piper's stomach to clench up again. *What is it with him?* she thought. *I can't put my finger on it*

"Long gone," he repeated, making it sound rather sinister. "Yes, that's certainly true." His teeth expanded into long, slim points, and his eyes flashed a pinkish hue. Piper shook her head, feeling as though she was hallucinating.

What the? . . . She wondered, suddenly dizzy.

Then everything went black.

The first thing Piper realized when she awoke was the soreness in her arms. She followed the sensation up and out to the extremities of her wrists and fingers, realizing without any great surprise that her arms were chained above her head. She gave an experimental tug. *Ow.* The chains, in addition to being snug, were not budging one bit. They were clearly cemented into the stone wall that, near as she could tell, she seemed to be pressed against. A gingerly effort to move her legs revealed that they, too, were shackled to the walls. The walls themselves were low and covered in mold, suggesting that wherever she was, it wasn't quite the Four Seasons.

This was not good.

"Ah, you're up," said a voice. Piper whipped her head around in the direction from which the voice had come—okay, so she still had range of motion there, that was something—to see Caitlyn, the elf nanny, glaring at her steadily.

"What's going on?" Piper asked. Her voice sounded small and groggy to her ears as it echoed through the tiny chamber.

"Well, you killed Mya, but as we said, that didn't really do us any good in the long run. The demon who's after our babies isn't going to stop just because she's been destroyed," Caitlyn said flatly.

"But, we told you we were going to help you!" Piper protested incredulously. "My husband is with the Elders right now! And Phoebe is at home looking through the Book of Shadows! We're going to get to the bottom of this."

"It's too late for that now," Caitlyn replied gravely. "The demon Lexor will not be put off. He came last night for the babies."

Piper felt a wave of guilt at not having been able to come up with a solution sooner. If the elves hadn't stolen Wyatt, would she have been motivated to move more quickly? There was no way to know, really. But they'd jeopardized her baby! Could anyone blame her for feeling slightly conflicted?

Yes, obviously, someone could. The elves could, for example. Caitlyn's face was a flat landscape of passivity, revealing zero emotion.

"He didn't take them, did he?" Piper asked nervously.

Caitlyn shook her head. "No, we were able to convince him to leave them be." Piper sighed with relief. "Of course, it was at no small price," the elf continued.

Piper surveyed her surroundings once more: a small, stone-walled hovel. Chains. And a very ill-tempered nanny as a guard. Realization dawned on her. "The price. The price was me," Piper said, piecing it all together.

"The demon wasn't keen to let go of his

plans for building an army," Caitlyn explained. "However, we convinced him that with you on his trail, the Charmed Ones were the most pressing threat. In exchange for leaving our babies alone, we promised to deliver you to him, breaking up the Power of Three and leaving him free to find another flock of children for his army."

Piper's mind raced. "Caitlyn, let's work together on this," she pleaded. "We can defeat him if we join forces. Tell me about Lexor. I don't know anything about him—"

"Because you dragged your heels," Caitlyn broke in. Piper sighed. Caitlyn wasn't entirely wrong. Still, she had to get the elf to free her— any way she could. *Maybe logic will work*, she thought.

"He should be the one you chain to this wall," Piper said. "Caitlyn, he's a *demon*. And I hate to break it to you, but most demons aren't exactly trustworthy. Which means that once the Power of Three has been broken, he's free to do as he pleases. Including taking your children again. *And* destroying you."

"Why would he do that?" Caitlyn asked. "What would he gain?"

"What can I tell you? Demons are wacky that way," Piper said. "They don't always play fair." She rattled her arms in their chains. Nothing doing. Firm as ever. "Your only hope is to let me out of here so my sisters and I can help you."

Caitlyn's expression was grim. "Even if I wanted to—which, for the record, I don't," she said emphatically, "I wouldn't be able to. Those chains are enchanted. I don't have the power to break them."

"Someone in your village must," Piper said, practically begging.

"But that's just it, Piper. We're nowhere near my village," Caitlyn said sweetly. "We're in Lexor's dungeon. He'll be here any minute. You're trapped in the Underworld, my dear."

Chapter Nine

"Paige! Thank goodness you're home!" Phoebe cried, leaping up from the couch and rushing to greet her sister.

"Okay . . . ," Paige said, slightly puzzled. "What's up?"

"I'm not sure," Phoebe said, stepping back and allowing Paige to catch her breath. "It's just, it's already—what time is it?" she asked, slightly frantic.

Paige gave Phoebe a puzzled look and raised her wrist to look at her watch. "Seven. So, yeah, I was a little late in leaving the center. Jonathan's father had a meeting or something, showed up half an hour after we closed."

"It's Piper," Phoebe explained. "She was supposed to be home around five. And I haven't heard from her."

Paige shrugged. "Maybe she's still meeting with that band manager. Wasn't she trying to

126

line up that group Pretty Little Devils?"

"It was just scheduling," Phoebe sa..
"There's no reason that should run so late. No
to mention, Piper would *never* be two hours late
without calling. It's not in her blood. *And* I practically had to shove her out of the house away
from Wyatt. She was going to rush right back to
see him. It just doesn't add up."

"Did you call her?" Paige asked.

Phoebe exhaled deeply. "A hundred times. Or,
at least five. It just goes straight to voice mail."

"Okay, well *that's* not Piper at all," Paige
agreed. "Have you left the house for any reason?
Is there any chance that she left a message on the
answering machine or something while you
were in the shower?"

Phoebe nodded her head, looking miserable.
"No, I was on that couch all afternoon. I finally
had an idea for my column, and I was writing the
whole time." She pointed at her humming laptop.

"Well, that's good news, anyway," Paige
quipped, trying to find a bright side. Phoebe
glared at her.

Paige dug into her bag and fished out her cell
phone. "She didn't leave me a message," she
confirmed after a quick scan of her screen. "I
agree. This is officially weird."

"So what do we do?" Phoebe asked. "Call
Leo?"

Paige shrugged. "I hate to disturb him if
we're not sure something's wrong."

Yeah, but I hate to just wait around doing
⁀hing if there *is* something wrong," Phoebe
⁀untered. "You're half Whitelighter. Can you
⁀ense her at all?"

Standing in the doorway between the hallway
and the living room, Paige stood stock still, letting
her arms hang at her sides. She closed her eyes and
concentrated on *feeling* Piper's essence filter into
her mind. She took a few deep breaths. Nothing.
After a moment she opened her eyes again, casting
a baleful look at her sister. "Nothing."

"Okay, more weird," Phoebe said. "If you
can't sense her, then she's off the radar, and
that's never good." She leaned back and took a
deep breath herself, preparing to call for her
brother-in-law. But before she could, the room
was bathed in shimmering white orbs as he
materialized right in the middle of the hallway.

"Leo!" Paige exclaimed. "We were just about
to call you."

"It's—," Phoebe began.

"Piper," Leo said, cutting her off. "She's disappeared. Completely off the radar." He looked
at the sisters grimly. "I guess this means you
haven't heard from her?"

"No, and I can't sense her either," Paige said,
sounding desperate. "That can't be good."

"What time was she supposed to come
home?" Leo asked.

"She told me she had to check on a couple of
things and meet with a band manager, and she'd

be home at five," Phoebe said. "She *really* didn't want to leave Wyatt alone for even that long." In his playpen Wyatt began to cry at the sound of his name. Phoebe picked him up and rocked him gently until he quieted.

"Piper would never be this late without calling—especially with you home watching Wyatt," Leo said, thinking out loud.

"Yeah, that was our conclusion too," Paige agreed. "So, can *you* sense her?"

Leo shook his head. "No. And the Elders aren't sure either. They sent me back down because they sensed something was going on."

"So you've got no new info on the demon that was bugging the elves?" Paige asked. This was going from bad to worse. Piper was gone, and they had no new information about who or what was after them.

"There's a chance that it's the demon Lexor. He was a former demonic general whose job was to lead an army of apocalyptic foot soldiers. But a century ago a group of good witches—your ancestors, in fact—destroyed his team. They weren't able to vanquish him, though. Ever since then he's been hell-bent on raising a new cadre. He's tried recruiting, but without great success."

"So he moved on to stealing babies and raising them as his own army," Paige guessed.

Leo shook his head. "We can't be sure, but it would make sense, wouldn't it?"

"Where can we find him?" Phoebe asked quietly.

"Well," Leo said slowly, "his lair is down in the Underworld. Which is dangerous enough. But I really don't think it's such a good idea to race off down there before we're sure that he's really the one."

"Oh, I'm feeling pretty sure," Phoebe said gravely. She bit her lip. "Leo, if you can't sense Piper, then she must be down in the Underworld, right?"

"Most likely, yes," Leo replied, his forehead creased in concern.

"So either way, whether it's Lexor or some-one—or some*thing*—else, we have to go down there. We have to get her back. And the longer we wait, the more danger she may be in," Phoebe said. She looked at Paige. "Right?"

Paige nodded slowly. "She has a point, Leo."

"True, but girls, we can't know what to expect when we don't even know who it is we're fac-ing. Best-case scenario is that it's Lexor, and we've got a little background on him. But that's *best* case. And keep in mind that your ancestors weren't able to vanquish him," he said, his voice solemn.

"Leo, you're missing the point," Phoebe argued. "Your best-case scenario is *our* best chance. And we have to take it."

Leo ran his fingers through his hair contem-platively. "I don't like it. But I agree—we can't leave Piper down there indefinitely." He looked dubiously at the girls. "And once we find her, we've got the Power of Three on our side." He sighed. "I just hate the idea of going down there totally unprepared."

Phoebe took a deep breath to respond, when she was suddenly wracked by a gripping spasm. Her mind went black, and then the darkness was replaced with a series of intercut images: *Piper chained to a wall—Caitlyn, the elf nanny, cowering in a corner—a burst of magic charge coming from . . . Wyatt? The sisters, hands joined, facing a tall, amorphous entity with slavering, quivering jowls and felinelike eyes.*

When the vision had passed, Phoebe opened her eyes to find Paige's arms around her waist, propping her up.

"What did you see?" Paige asked nervously.

"I know where she is," Phoebe said. "And I know who she's with. Leo, does Lexor have, um, sort of cat's eyes? And he's a big, blurry, dark shape, with slobbery teeth?"

Leo eyed Phoebe. "Unfortunately, yes. I'm guessing that means that's who has Piper."

Phoebe shuddered. "Yeah. Not gonna win any Underworld beauty contests, that's for sure. And Caitlyn's down there too. The elves must have made a deal with him: In exchange for him leaving their babies alone—they promised him one of us."

"To destroy the Power of Three, so he'd be

free to put together whatever army he wanted," Paige finished, piecing it all together. "So you saw us kicking his butt, right? Trouncing his sorry self all over the Underworld?"

"Um, I saw us *fighting* him," Phoebe hedged. "Obviously that means we're gonna win." She crossed her fingers surreptitiously behind her back.

"Then let's go," Paige said.

"One problem, folks," Leo pointed out. "I'm not letting you go by yourselves."

"We can handle it, Leo," Phoebe said, even though she wasn't quite sure she believed that.

"What if you need to be healed?" Leo said with total sincerity.

Phoebe put her hands on her hips, frustrated. "Fine. If you're going to use logic, I suppose I can't argue. Paige, why don't you run upstairs and see if there are any generic vanquishing potions in the attic?"

Paige raised a skeptical eyebrow at her sister. "I don't know if 'generic' is gonna do it for Mister Slobberjaw," she said tentatively.

"Power of Three," Phoebe reminded her.

"What about Wyatt?" Leo said, tense. "I'm not leaving him behind."

"That's not going to be a problem, actually," Phoebe said.

"You're not suggesting we bring him, are you?" Leo asked.

Phoebe shrugged. "We don't really have a

choice, do we? Anyway, according to my vision, he's coming along for the ride."

Orbing to the Underworld was an alarmingly straightforward process. It was a matter of moments before the group found itself knee-deep in a murky river, which unfortunately smelled like a cross between sewage and rotting vegetation. "Ugh, Leo," Phoebe said, wildly trying to breathe through her mouth, "you couldn't have orbed to some place slightly less . . . *septic*?"

"That's not *quite* how it works, Phoebe," he reminded her, and patted Wyatt, who was dangling from Leo's neck in a Snugli and appeared to be the only member of the group who was unfazed by the new surroundings.

"I'm just glad I was wearing my knee-high boots this morning," Paige joked, lifting one out of the water. Taking note of its soggy, water-logged condition, she wrinkled her nose and changed her mind. "Or maybe not." She paused, concentrating. "I can feel Piper," she said excitedly. "She's nearby. But it's faint. Can you tell where it's coming from, Leo?"

Leo frowned. "Like you said—it's nearby. But it's fuzzy, like a scrambled signal. Maybe Lexor has some sort of magical field around his lair?"

"In which case we're in trouble," Phoebe griped.

"Well, maybe—oh!" Paige began. She didn't

have time to complete her thought, however, before the group was suddenly swathed in white lights and whisked away into the ether.

They landed in a small, stone-walled room that was dank and musty. After they had all brushed themselves off from the unexpected travel, they took a look around. The first thing they noticed was Caitlyn, cowering in the corner.

The second thing they noticed was Piper.

"Piper!" Phoebe said, rushing toward her sister and enveloping her in the closest thing to a hug she could manage, considering the chains and the wall.

"How'd you guys find me?" Piper asked.

"I couldn't," Leo admitted, looking toward Paige.

"It wasn't me," Paige said simply. She pointed to Wyatt, bouncing contentedly against Leo's chest. "I guess there's a good reason we needed him along."

"That's my boy," Leo said proudly.

"Fools!" Caitlyn hissed from her perch in the corner. "Lexor is due to arrive. You're insane to think you can defeat him."

"Maybe," Piper agreed. She smiled. "But maybe not."

Before she could go on, a gust of wind filled the room. Suddenly a tornado-style funnel built up in the center of the tiny area, quickly growing larger and gathering momentum.

"Uh, this isn't looking so good," Paige shouted above the rush of the funnel, her hair whipping across her face angrily.

"Ya think?" Piper yelled back. She jerked her arms futilely, trying to break the chains, which held fast.

"Lexor approaches," Caitlyn called, sounding terrified.

The whirlwind built to a fever pitch and then dissipated, streaming through a crack in the stone ceiling. As the tornado cleared, Lexor himself was slowly revealed, a snarling, hunch-backed, slavering beast with sharklike rows of razor-sharp teeth, a hulking body covered in hair, and neon green eyes narrowed to tiny slits.

"WHERE IS SHE?" he bellowed to Caitlyn. "WHERE IS MY WITCH?"

With a squeak Caitlyn managed to gesture toward Piper, chained to the wall.

Lexor stood up straighter and lumbered over to Piper in two gigantic steps. He leaned over her, breathing heavily. "Wonderful," he declared. "The Power of Three, severed forever." He reached out an oversize paw toward her face.

Piper did her best not to shrink back in revulsion as his hand drew nearer. Just when his touch seemed as inevitable as his drool—*Ick*, she thought—she felt a tingle at her wrists and her arms fell to her sides.

"*Chains!*" Paige called commandingly, holding her arms out to receive them. The chains groaned and clanked, finally scraping free of the wall, sailing across the room into Paige's hands and trailing with them a good deal of mortar. Chunks of stone rained down on Piper and on Lexor, which didn't seem to make the demon especially happy. He reared up and roared, showering Piper in his wet, demony breath all over again.

"Oh, yuck, why is it demons have never heard of oral hygiene?" she said despairingly. She flattened herself against the wall, creating as much distance as possible between herself and the demon, then let loose. Lexor reeled back against the far wall with a resounding crash— but he didn't explode.

"*Dammit!*" Piper yelled. She looked at Wyatt guiltily. "I mean, *darn it!*"

By this point Caitlyn had curled herself into a tight, shivering ball in the corner of the room. Lexor saw her in his periphery and was engulfed in rage. "You promised me *one* witch!" he shouted, winding up and blasting her with an energy ball. Caitlyn squeezed her eyes shut but otherwise offered no defense. The energy ball hit her, and she slumped over like a rag doll.

"Caitlyn!" Paige shouted, rushing to her side. She grabbed the elf's tiny wrist. "Leo, there's no pulse."

"Paige, bigger problems," Phoebe warned as Lexor hauled off to launch another energy ball— this one straight at Paige's head. Piper reached out and intercepted it, exploding it in midair.

"The witches were supposed to be SEPA-RATED!" Lexor bellowed, pounding his fists against the walls in fury.

"Well, you got unlucky," Phoebe said flatly. "And bad luck always comes in threes." She sailed through the air and landed a flying kick directly in his neck. He collapsed, clutching his windpipe and gasping.

"Girls, the Power of Three," Leo reminded them anxiously.

"Oh, right," Phoebe said, rejoining her sisters and grabbing their hands. "This one's easy."

Hands joined, the sisters squared off against a weakened Lexor.

> "The Power of Three will set us free
> The Power of Three will set us free
> The Power of Three will set us free"

They chanted in unison, but it didn't seem to be having any effect. If anything, Lexor looked as if he was feeling a little better. And like he was a lot more pissed off.

"Uh, next idea?" Piper asked nervously.

"I'm not sure. We were convinced the whole Power of Three thing was gonna work," Paige admitted, not liking the looks of the situation.

Lexor grinned cunningly. "It looks like I needn't have bothered to split you up, precious Charmed Ones," he intoned nastily. "And now,

I can kill three birds with one stone."

Suddenly Phoebe remembered her vision and was hit with a flash of inspiration. "Paige, orb Wyatt! Orb Wyatt!" she cried frantically.

Paige held out her arms and called to him. "Wyatt!" she said. Once he was safely to her, she passed him to Piper. "A little extra boost from our Charmed baby," she explained, crossing her fingers behind her back that this would work. The girls clasped hands again.

"The Power of Three will set us free!"

They proclaimed it more forcefully this time. All at once, a powerful wave of energy came over them. The sisters' knees buckled and they staggered backward. The wall rippled forward, washing over Lexor. As it covered his body, his skin began to ripple and shred, finally disintegrating into a pile of ash. He opened his mouth wide to scream, but the acid-rain effect made its way up his body before he could utter a sound. With one final hum and one final pop, the wall closed in on itself, leaving nothing in its trace but the slight smell of gasoline and the tower of dust that had, moments before, been Lexor himself.

Paige sneezed. "Gross. I think I'm allergic to demon dust."

"Better than ragweed," Phoebe pointed out. "Less common during the summer season."

"Wyatt, you are such a good boy, such a patient boy, such a *powerful* boy," Piper cooed to her son, bouncing him in his Snugli and tickling him on the chin. "We couldn't have done it without you."

"That's for damn sure," Phoebe said, wiping a smudge of Lexor dust off her forehead. "Three cheers for motherhood!" She raised her well-toned arms in a victory salute.

"Uh, girls, Caitlyn's really not breathing," Paige said. She was crouched in the corner with the elf, who had taken on a slightly blue hue.

Leo plucked Wyatt from Piper's arms and carried him over to Paige. "Since his input was so helpful during the last go-round, why not give this guy another chance to save the day?" he suggested. Paige wrapped one arm around Wyatt's stomach and balanced him on her knee. She took his little hand and held it, clasped in her own, over Caitlyn's prone body. Slowly a bright glow began to emanate from their grip. It grew larger, washing over the elf's body, until she sat up, coughing, and blinked at Paige. "You saved me," she marveled. "Even after everything that's happened."

Paige tilted her head toward Wyatt, who was grinning broadly. "Really, it was him. Apparently he doesn't hold a grudge."

"I'm truly grateful," Caitlyn replied, sounding sincere.

"Are you feeling up to a little travel?" Piper

asked. "We'll take you back to your village."

"You'd do that?" Caitlyn asked in disbelief. "Even after everything the elves have done? All of the trouble we've caused you?"

"Well, yes, but we do have an ulterior motive," Paige clarified.

Caitlyn nodded resignedly. "I can't say I'm surprised," she said. She brushed herself off and got to her feet. She looked at the girls, her expression one of grim determination. "Let's go, then," she said.

They huddled together and orbed off to the elf village.

Rowan, the elf king, seemed inordinately surprised to find the Charmed Ones standing before him on the royal carpet. "Er, hi," he managed to choke out after a moment of agonizingly awkward silence. "How's it going?"

"You'll be happy to know that we took care of your demon," Phoebe said, glaring at him. "Lexor's gone. If you had just given us some time, he would have been anyway, and Piper wouldn't have been endangered, and Caitlyn wouldn't have gotten hurt."

Caitlyn hung her head, ashamed. "It's true, Rowan. The girls saved me from Lexor. We should have trusted them. We shouldn't have made deals with a demon."

"Good rule of thumb, as a matter of fact," Piper put in.

"All's well that ends well, then?" Rowan hedged.

"Not quite, buddy," Piper said, shaking her head.

"See, we know that elves aren't really creatures of evil, inherently," Paige explained. "But you guys . . . ," she trailed off uncertainly.

"Maybe it's because you're out here in the woods, sequestered from other elves and magic users, but, let's just say, based on the way you've been behaving lately, we think you've gone a little nuts," Piper said.

"We mean that in as nice a way as possible!" Phoebe offered. "But, yeah. Stealing human babies to pawn off on a demon army, consorting with a demon to break up the Charmed Ones—it's not looking so good for your case."

"What will you do to us?" Rowan asked, frightened. He finally seemed to grasp the gravity of the situation.

"We're not out to get you, but we do have to put a stop to you," Piper explained. "Ergo, we're gonna have to bind your powers."

"We won't have powers?" Caitlyn gasped.

"We're not stripping them, just binding them," Piper said carefully. "And just the ones that allow you to do anything to humans . . . or to us."

"You wouldn't be able to bind *all* of our powers," Rowan countered darkly.

"Wanna bet?" Paige asked. "But we won't. We would never leave you defenseless. Assembly room!" she called, closing her eyes and orbing them all off.

When she opened her eyes again, she and her sisters found themselves gathered at the front of the elves' assembly hall, surrounded by confused-looking creatures. A low hush of worried whispers filled the hall.

"Piper, freeze them!" Phoebe suggested.

"Oh, right. Good thinking," Piper said, flicking her wrists and effectively putting the room on pause. She turned to her sister. "Have you got a binding spell?"

Phoebe looked at Piper, wide eyed. "Um, how about . . ." She wracked her brain wildly. "Oh!

> *"Magic creatures of the woods,*
> *Rose against the cause of good.*
> *To help our kind in this dire hour,*
> *We witches bind these certain powers!"*

She looked up at her sisters proudly. "Good?"

Paige indicated a little ripple of magic, almost like a heatwave, rolling across the rows of elves. "Looks like it worked," she said.

Piper reached out and unfroze the room. Rowan immediately reached out toward the sisters to perform some sort of indeterminate magic. A small popping sound emanated from his wrists, but nothing else. He tried the same motion toward an innocent elf, who immediately turned into a small rabbit. Sighing disgustedly, Rowan changed the bunny back into a boy elf.

The sisters exchanged a satisfied glance. "It definitely worked," Piper said.

"You can't do this!" Rowan cried, furious, jumping up and down and stamping his feet.

"We can, we have, we're going," Phoebe countered.

"I think, given everything that's gone down, you all got off pretty easy," Paige commented. She found Caitlyn in the room and made eye contact. "And you . . . I'd better not find you working any more child-care gigs, okay?"

Caitlyn nodded shortly, chastised.

Leo put his arms out, gathering the sisters to him. "Are we ready to go back to the Manor?" he asked.

All three girls looked at him with a mixture of exhaustion and eagerness. "Yes, *please*," they said simultaneously. From his Snugli on Leo's chest, Wyatt giggled at their impromptu singsong, and the group orbed back to the Manor, leaving Rowan and his kingdom to deal with their frustration on their own.

Chapter Ten

When Paige arrived at the Bayside Child Care Center the next morning, she wasn't surprised to find the infant room filled to capacity again. "They're all back!" she exclaimed happily to Dori. "Fabulous!"

Dori beamed beatifically, balancing one baby over each shoulder. She seemed positively thrilled at this turn of events. "Yes, they were all brought in first thing this morning. No real explanation given, but everyone's parents said they were acting like themselves again. I was afraid the parents wouldn't want to put their children back in child care here, but I guess it just goes to show that at the end of the day they *do* trust us!"

"I guess so," Paige said, smiling. She was glad to see that her boss's confidence had been restored. Paige was in such a good mood, in fact, that she thought she might stop by the local surf shop after work. She did still have Drew's card, after all.

"And something else, too!" Dori continued, breaking into Paige's happy reverie. "I hired someone new!"

Paige's nerves went into high alert. "How did you find her?" she asked instantly.

"It's a him, actually. I found him through a temp agency, like you. We met last night for an interview, after you'd gone home. He's getting his degree in elementary education, which is so unusual for a man, don't you think?"

"Yes, it is," Paige agreed, hoping that in this case "unusual" wouldn't turn out to equal "black magic."

"And he'll be great around here, because he's so incredibly tall!" Dori continued. "I think six-two, or six-four! Finally, someone to change all of the lightbulbs!" she trilled enthusiastically.

Paige sighed with relief. *At least I can rule out psycho elves*, she thought. *That's something.* She patted Dori on the back encouragingly, then made her way over to one of the worktables where Natalie was sitting alone, drawing.

Paige slid into the seat next to her. "How are you today, Natalie?"

Natalie looked over to Paige questioningly. "You mean am I glad because the real babies are back?"

"Well, actually, it was more of a general question, but sure," Paige replied. "You must be."

Natalie nodded. "And I'm glad the scary nurse is gone."

"Me too," Paige agreed. "And she isn't coming back, I can promise you that. And you should know something, Natalie," Paige continued. "I would never have known what was wrong with the babies if it wasn't for your help. So I don't want you ever to think there's anything wrong with your 'imagination.' If there are people who don't like to hear about it, well, I can't really do anything about that, but I *can* promise you that there are people who will always listen to what you have to say. And believe you. People like me."

Natalie's eyes filled with tears, and she put down her crayons and threw her arms around Paige's neck. At that moment Paige never wanted to work anywhere else. "Thank you," Natalie whispered fiercely. "Thank you, Paige."

"Thank you, Phoebe," Elise was saying, standing in the doorway of Phoebe's office. "Thank you so much for that column! What can I say? It was . . . inspired. Truly."

Phoebe shrugged modestly, aiming for nonchalant and not quite making it. *So what?* she thought. *I busted my butt coming up with that idea!* "It just came to me," she explained. "I had gotten so many letters about new babies from different mothers, and I started to wish I could get them in one room to exchange ideas. It seemed like the most comprehensive solution. I mean, *they're* the experts with hands-on experience, not me. No matter how many auntie hours I log."

"Well, you should know that the phone's been ringing off the hook with calls from readers who *love* your idea. Honestly—an I-community! For mommies! A site where moms can post and chat in real time! It's so perfect, I don't know why it took us so long to come up with it!"

"Us?" Phoebe asked.

"Well, you," Elise amended, waving her hand in Phoebe's direction. "But here's the thing. We're going to get our tech team to build a sub-site on our own Web site for your I-community. And we want *you* to oversee the content."

Phoebe gasped with delight. "Mom-to-mom?"

"Mom-to-mom, girlfriend-to-girlfriend, student-to-student . . . The sky's the limit, Phoebe. It's your baby. That is, if you want it."

Phoebe jumped up from her desk with joy. "Are you kidding? A whole new section of the Web site—all mine? Of *course* I want it! Elise, thank you so much!" she gushed.

"You don't have to thank me, Phoebe—though of course I appreciate it," Elise said. "This one was all yours."

After Elise had walked away, Phoebe allowed herself a moment to bask in the praise. The idea *had* been all hers, after all. She may not have known the answers to all of the new moms' problems, but she knew how to help them find them. She loved her job, and she was good at it too. She was a good aunt to Wyatt, and a good protector of Innocents. And when the time came for her to take the plunge into motherhood herself, well . . . she had a feeling she'd be pretty good at that, too.

"Piper, are you *sure* about this?" Leo pressed for what seemed like the millionth time.

Piper placed her hands on her hips and squared off against her husband. "Yes, I am sure. I could not be more sure. If the sure police were riding through San Francisco, they'd arrest me for toxic levels of sureness."

Leo smiled. "Okay. Just checking."

"And double-checking, and triple-checking," Piper said, grinning at him. She leaned away from the sink, where she was in the middle of rinsing the breakfast dishes, and gave him a quick kiss on the cheek. "I am going to channel my inner Martha again," she insisted. "I am going to cook, clean, and care for my son."

"It's a good plan, sweetie," Leo agreed. "But I'm worried that you're going to go a little bit stir crazy. Like we discussed last time—"

"Right, and remember how well *that* worked out?" Piper reminded him. "Wyatt was a changeling and every time I went into the club for one reason or another I ended up distracted, disengaged, or in danger!"

Leo sighed wearily. "Yes, I remember," he

conceded. "I'm not going to try to talk you in or out of any decisions. But I *will* stick around this afternoon in case you need anything."

"I will be *fine*," she insisted. "After I finish with the dishes, I'm going to bake some cornbread for dinner. And the gardener's coming to refertilize the front lawn. It's all under control."

Leo nodded. "You are a true domestic goddess," he said. "I'll just be upstairs reading, then."

As Leo slipped upstairs, Piper turned back to the dishes, humming softly to herself under her breath. She was glad to have an afternoon at home with her baby. The whole balancing-act thing was really stressful and, as she'd just illuminated for Leo, hadn't been working out for her so well of late. So for today, she'd just load up the dishwasher, then bake some—just then Wyatt began to cry.

She turned and was horrified when she tripped and spilled the bag of cornmeal. Wyatt was covered in it, not to mention gleefully plunging his hands into a mountain of it that had landed on his bouncy chair. The bag itself lay overturned on the floor, spilling grainy powder all across the tiles. "Wyatt!" Piper shrieked, running to him and frantically trying to scoop up the mess with her hands.

Unfortunately, in her haste and horror, she'd forgotten to take off her rubber gloves. Now the cornmeal was sticking to her wet, latex-encased hands in thick chunks. Not good.

The sound of water dribbling onto the floor reminded Piper that she also hadn't turned off the faucet. She scrambled back to the sink and quickly twisted the tap, leaving a clump of wet cornmeal stuck to it. She turned and leaned her back against the sink. "Crisis averted," she said to Wyatt, who seemed to find the whole thing utterly hysterical. "Yeah, yeah, it's a laugh riot," she said wearily. She turned to reach for a sponge and slipped on the wet floor. She went down like a ton of bricks.

At that moment the doorbell rang. "Gardener!" Piper heard from the direction of the front door. She paused for a moment, trying to gather her composure. The doorbell rang again, this time more insistently. Then the gardener began to knock loudly.

A shimmer of white lights signaled Leo's return to the kitchen. "Piper, didn't you hear the gardener . . ." He trailed off when he saw her sitting cross-legged in a puddle surrounded by drying heaps of cornmeal. "Oh," he said quickly. "I'll just show the gardener around the back."

"Would you? That'd be fab," Piper said, trying hard to keep the edge out of her voice.

She had managed to gingerly pull herself back into an upright position and peel off the rubber gloves, when Leo returned from leading the gardener to the backyard. "Are you hurt?" he asked, giving her a quick once-over.

She shook her head no. "Just my pride, a little."

She looked around at the mess the kitchen had become. "A lot," she admitted.

Leo took her hands in his own and looked into her eyes. "You know, Piper, I think there's another glass shipment coming into P3 this afternoon. Around three o'clock. It should only take an hour or two. I bet the evening manager would be glad to have you around to supervise."

Piper raised an eyebrow at her husband. "Oh, do you think?" she asked, a twinkle in her eyes.

"Piper, I don't think there's such a thing as 'having it all,'" Leo said softly. "But if you're so hell-bent on trying, I'd say the first step is probably looking for a little balance."

"You told me I needed to stop thinking in black-and-white terms," Piper reminded him. "I think you were on to something."

"You're saying you're ready for shades of gray?" Leo asked in mock disbelief.

"I'm saying"—Piper's gaze swept the minefield of the kitchen once more—"I'm saying the grayer, the better. I'm saying I'm going to go oversee that shipment at P3, for a while, if you're okay to watch Wyatt."

"More than okay," Leo said, kissing the tip of her nose. "Glad to do it."

"Mmmm," Piper responded, kissing him deeply. "And one other thing."

"Anything you want," Leo said. "Say the word."

Piper looked up at him. She gestured to the room.

"Promise me you'll clean the kitchen while I'm gone."

At that, Leo swatted Piper playfully on the shoulder, causing the two of them to dissolve in laughter. Wyatt seemed to find this all endlessly amusing, and he, too, joined in on the giggle fest. The sound was music to Piper's ears. *I'll be Home Piper for now,* she decided. *And then I'll go be the other Piper, the Working Piper, for a little while. And then I'll come home again. I'm gonna have to learn to compromise a little if I want this to work—and if I want to maintain my sanity.*

Listening to Leo's laughter mingling with Wyatt's, Piper suddenly realized that compromise was just fine. No—it was better than fine. In fact, it was exactly what she needed.

About the Author

Micol Ostow is a writer and editor of books for children, tweens, and teens. She lives and works (but rarely sleeps) in New York City.

Charmed

"We're the protectors of the innocent.
We're known as the Charmed Ones."

—Phoebe Halliwell, "Something Wicca This Way Comes"

Go behind the scenes of television's sexiest supernatural thriller with *The Book of Three*, the *only* fully authorized companion to the witty, witchy world of *Charmed*!

Published by Simon & Schuster

Charmed.

"We all need to believe that magic exists."
—Phoebe Halliwell, "Trial by Magic"

When Phoebe Halliwell returned to San Francisco to live with her older sisters, Prue and Piper, in Halliwell Manor, she had no idea the turn her life—*all* their lives—would take. Because when Phoebe found the Book of Shadows in the Manor's attic, she learned that she and her sisters were the Charmed Ones, the most powerful witches of all time. Battling demons, warlocks, and other black-magic baddies, Piper and Phoebe lost Prue but discovered their long-lost half-Whitelighter, half-witch sister, Paige Matthews. The Power of Three was reborn.

Look for a new Charmed novel every other month!